Wizards
OF WAVERLY PLACE

OF WAVERLY PLACE

Once Upon a Vampire

Adapted by Ellie O'Ryan

Based on the series created by Todd J. Greenwald

Part One is based on the episode "Justin & Juliet," Written by Peter Murrieta

Part Two is based on the episode "Healthy Eating," Written by Justin Varava

Part Three is based on the episode "Wake Up, Break Up, Shake Up," Written by Gigi McCreery & Perry Rein

Part Four is based on the episode "No Fear," Written by Gigi McCreery & Perry Rein

DISNEP PRESS

New York

PART
ONE

Chapter One

In the heart of New York City's Greenwich Village, the Waverly Sub Station—a fantastic sandwich shop in an old subway car, run by the Russo family—was quiet. Surprisingly quiet, in fact, considering that it was dinnertime.

Justin and Max Russo tried to keep busy by slowly wiping off tables that were already clean. Their mother, Theresa, rearranged the condiments on each table—again. And their dad, Jerry, frowned at the clock.

"Where is everybody?" he asked. "This is the slowest dinner rush we've ever had."

"The city must have taken down your Last Sandwich for Forty Miles sign," Justin joked.

Max rolled his eyes and blew a straw wrapper at his big brother.

Just then, a bell jangled as someone opened the door. The whole family turned, ready to welcome a customer at last.

But it wasn't a customer. It was just Alex Russo, Justin and Max's sister. She was chowing down on a large sandwich.

"This sandwich is amazing!" Alex raved, closing her eyes blissfully. "It's smoked turkey with pesto mayonnaise and some kind of fancy cheese. I know it was fancy because they didn't spray it on!"

"Where did you get that?" Mr. Russo asked, narrowing his eyes suspiciously. He knew one thing: that tasty-sounding sandwich hadn't been made in the kitchen of the Waverly Sub Station.

Alex didn't answer right away. She pointed to her mouth, which was full of a bite of sandwich. There was silence as everyone waited for her to swallow. Finally, she said, "It's from a new place down the street—the Late Nite Bite. It's superclose. We can go there all the time! The only problem is that it's always packed." Alex paused as she glanced around the empty restaurant. "Not like this place."

A frown crossed Mrs. Russo's face. "There's another sandwich shop on Waverly Place?" she asked. "That sounds like competition."

"There's no competition," Mr. Russo said confidently. He knew that he made delicious sandwiches—after all, the Waverly Sub Station had never had problems drumming up business before. "Let me taste that," Mr. Russo continued as he reached for Alex's sandwich.

Grabbing it before his daughter could protest, Mr. Russo chomped down on the sandwich. He wanted to hate it. He wanted it to be the foulest food ever created. But it was not to be. Mr. Russo grinned. "Mmmm!" he exclaimed, savoring the perfect blend of seasonings. Then he remembered where the sandwich had come from: someone else's restaurant. "I mean, there's no competition," he repeated.

Max jumped up and grabbed the sandwich away from his dad. He took a big bite. "Mmmm!" He echoed Mr. Russo. "This sandwich is better than pizza! But don't tell pizza I said that. She gets so jealous."

"Oh, great," Alex said, rolling her eyes at her little—and in her opinion, annoying—brother. "Your first serious relationship is with my sandwich. Give it back!"

She reached for her sandwich, but Mrs. Russo beat her to it. "Jerry, maybe we should send someone down there to check them out," she said, sounding worried. Then Mrs. Russo took a bite of the sandwich and her eyes went all dreamy. "I'll go!" she exclaimed. It was clear she just wanted to get her own delicious sandwich from the Late Nite Bite.

"No, *I'll* go, because I need a new sandwich," Alex replied, patting her still-too-empty stomach.

"We only send you on missions of destruction," Mr. Russo said playfully as he put his arm around Alex's shoulders. "Max we send to confuse people. For research and surveillance, Justin is our guy!"

"Cool!" Justin said excitedly. "I've got just the decoy. I'll speak in my Australian accent!" He strutted around the restaurant, practicing his best Australian accent. "I'd like to try your shrimp-on-the-barbie sandy-wich, mate!"

Max raised an eyebrow. "That is *not* an Australian accent," he announced. "Now, *I* am a master of voices. Listen!" Max took a deep breath and said, "I'd like to try your shrimp-on-the-barbie sandy-wich, mate!"

Max had confidence, and he definitely had style. The only problem was that his accent sounded more like Jim Carrey than someone from Australia!

Justin rolled his eyes. "That's not an accent. That's your lame Jim Carrey impression!" he retorted.

"Yes, but you knew who it was," Max pointed out, unfazed. "I'm going to be in my one-man show when school starts. I'm going to work on my impressions all summer!"

"All summer, huh?" Alex asked. She did *not* sound happy to hear that. In fact, her head already ached from thinking about Max parading around—doing voices—for all those months.

Max put on a pair of sunglasses and flashed Alex a big smile. "All work and no play makes

Jack a dull boy," he said in a gravelly voice. Then, in his regular voice, Max explained, "Jack Nicholson."

Alex groaned. "All summer with no Max would make Alex a happy girl," she told her brother. "That was Alex Russo!"

The Russo kids teased each other a lot, but in reality, they were really tight. You kind of had to be when you shared a secret like theirs. It was a *big* secret.

Alex, Justin, and Max were all wizards and had magical powers that they had inherited from their dad. Almost no one outside the Russo family knew about them—especially not the other kids at school, or the customers who usually stopped into the Waverly Sub Station for a quick bite to eat.

Mr. Russo had been forced to give up his magical powers when he fell in love and married Mrs. Russo, because she wasn't a wizard. Even so, all three kids were born with some pretty impressive magical talents.

Mrs. Russo wanted her kids to lead magic-free lives as much as possible. She thought it was important for them to have normal lives. But both the Russo parents agreed that their kids needed to learn how to use their powers wisely.

In wizard families, all the kids got their powers when they turned twelve. But the rule was that only one child in each family could keep his or her powers when they became adults. The kid who performed magic the best, won the title of family wizard. It was up to Mr. Russo to teach them everything he knew about magic. So, twice a week after school he gave Alex, Justin, and Max top-secret magic lessons in the basement, which they called the Wizard's Lair.

Mr. and Mrs. Russo had always been very clear with their kids: no unsupervised magic. Ever! But sometimes it wasn't easy for the kids to resist the urge to do magic—especially when it made life so much easier, *and* so much more interesting. All the Russo kids loved to learn new techniques, but Alex's daring personality and impulsive nature meant that her magic experiments often led to trouble. Max, the youngest Russo sibling, still had a lot to learn before his magical powers would catch up to his older brother and sister's skills. Dependable, reliable Justin was more careful—but he was always quick to help out if Alex got in a jam.

It was precisely because of his cautious nature that Justin was the perfect choice to go on an undercover mission to the Late Nite Bite. If any of the Russos could spy on the competition without getting caught—or even noticed—it would be Justin.

"Just get their menu and come back," Mrs. Russo advised Justin as he put on his coat.

"And try to get their recipe for pesto

mayonnaise, too," Mr. Russo added, licking his fingers.

Mrs. Russo frowned. "Just the menu," she repeated. "Don't get caught. And be careful!"

Justin gave his family a confident wave as he walked out of the restaurant. He appreciated their advice—but he knew that his Australian accent would make the perfect disguise. No one would be able to tell it was fake—or figure out that Justin wasn't who he appeared to be! This mission would be a breeze.

Chapter Two

Justin walked down the crowded sidewalk toward the Late Nite Bite. He passed by the groups of students and artists who loved to hang out in Greenwich Village, one of the coolest neighborhoods in New York City. But he didn't get distracted. He remained focused—like a superspy. Nothing could stop him. Although those sunglasses looked pretty cool . . . He shook his head and refocused.

It wasn't hard to find the restaurant that had stolen the Waverly Sub Station's clients—there was a long line of people snaking out the front door. Justin casually walked down a flight of stairs and slipped into the sandwich shop, ready to begin surveillance.

The Late Nite Bite was a small restaurant, located in a dark, windowless basement. Despite the lack of light, it was packed, with every table filled and a small crowd of people waiting to order sandwiches. Justin pulled out his cameraphone and started to record some video of the restaurant.

"As expected, the place is very busy," Justin said, speaking in a quiet voice that was just loud enough for the cameraphone's recorder to pick up. "Ah-ha! They're open twenty-four hours. I don't know why I said 'Ah-ha.' Let's see . . . here is one of their menus."

Justin opened the folded paper menu and began to record it with his cameraphone.

Just then, a beautiful girl crossed the restaurant. She had shiny blond hair and very pale skin. To Justin's surprise, she stopped when she reached him—and gave him a shy smile.

"You know those are take-out menus," she said in a friendly tone. "If you want a copy of it, the trash can out front probably has about twenty of them."

That had been close! But Justin wasn't worried. He smiled confidently and said, in his best Australian accent, "I take photographs of menus. I'm an artist. An Australian menu artist. Love your variety of sandy-wiches!"

The girl laughed. "Oh, I was so on board with your whole Australian thing until you said 'sandy-wiches,'" she teased.

Justin dropped the accent at once. "They don't say that?" he asked, his brown eyes suddenly filled with concern.

"No," the girl said. "But they really say

15

things like 'dingo,' 'koala,' and 'boomerang,' which is usually followed by 'Duck!'"

"I'm sorry," Justin said. He couldn't believe his accent had failed him—and blown his cover!

"Don't be sorry," the girl said as she flashed Justin a dazzling smile. "I like fake accents. I also like fake mustaches."

"Oh, my gosh!" Justin exclaimed. "I have one! I *knew* I should have worn it!"

"Um, it's okay," the girl said. "I was kind of kidding."

Justin smiled back at her. "I'm Justin," he said.

"I'm Juliet Van Heusen," the girl replied. "Do you want to hear about our special?"

Justin raised an eyebrow. "I think I'm looking at it," he said. "Ooh, was that smooth?"

"Yes—but you ruined it by talking about it," Juliet said. "But you're still cute."

Before Justin could respond to Juliet's compliment, a pair of adults—her parents—approached them. They were both dressed in rather formal clothing and had the same pale skin as their daughter.

"Juliet, you didn't tell us we had a special visitor," Mr. Van Heusen said smoothly as he reached out to shake Justin's hand. "Pardon me. Aren't you the young man who works at Waverly Sub Station?"

"I got a sandwich there last week," Mrs. Van Heusen said. "I was on a bland diet, and you guys really got me through it." She smiled at Justin, but like her false compliment, her smile wasn't genuine at all. Not like Juliet's pretty grin.

"Hi, I'm Justin Russo," Justin replied as he introduced himself. Despite her coldness, he knew he needed to get in good with Mrs. Van Heusen. He figured her approval would be important if he wanted to spend more time with Juliet. Which he did—most definitely. "Lovely dress. By the way, I've always thought that people should dress up to make sandwiches. Out of respect to the profession of sandwich-making."

Mr. Van Heusen knew exactly what Justin was up to. "Insincere compliments!" he announced. "Well, I see the game is afoot."

"Insincere?" Mrs. Van Heusen snapped. "I knew you didn't like this dress!"

"Juliet," Mr. Van Heusen continued, "this boy is here to spy on our establishment."

"He's not spying, Daddy," Juliet replied at once. "He's very nice. He was just videotaping the menu for his . . ." Juliet's voice trailed off as she realized what she was saying. Then she exclaimed, "Oh, my gosh! He might have been spying!"

Mr. Van Heusen didn't miss a beat. "I'm afraid, Justin Russo, that I'm going to have to ask you to leave. If you don't, the consequences will be most horrible and permanent!" He thrust his hands toward Justin and waved his fingers strangely.

Mrs. Van Heusen put her hand on her husband's arm. "Honey, what did we say about the hand gestures?" she asked gently.

"Not in the restaurant," Mr. Van Heusen replied with a sigh. He wished his wife would understand that his threats weren't nearly as scary without the hand gestures!

"That's right," Mrs. Van Heusen said encouragingly.

Juliet grabbed Justin by the sleeve and pulled him over toward the door. "Here, take this," she whispered as she pressed a small slip of paper into his hand.

"But this has someone's phone number on it," Justin replied, confused.

"Yeah. It's the cute girl who works at the Late Nite Bite," Juliet replied with a wink.

"Ooooh!" Justin exclaimed as he realized

that Juliet was giving him *her* phone number. "I like her!"

As Justin winked back, Mr. Van Heusen yelled, "Juliet, stop talking to Justin Russo and banish him from our castle! And by castle, I mean our subterranean eatery!"

Justin ran out the door and leaped up the stairs, taking them two at a time. He was in such a rush that he didn't even notice when Mr. Van Heusen did those weird hand gestures again. And he didn't notice when Mrs. Van Heusen scolded her husband again, yelling, "Hands!"

But he *did* notice that Mr. Van Heusen had called the Late Nite Bite his castle. And that seemed very strange indeed.

Chapter Three

When Justin got back to the Waverly Sub Station, Mr. and Mrs. Russo closed the restaurant to hold an important family meeting. Normally, Mr. Russo would never have allowed the restaurant to close during the dinner rush—but he figured it was okay just this once, since they didn't have any customers anyway.

The whole family waited expectantly as

Justin rolled a large whiteboard into the middle of the restaurant. There was silence as he covered the board with writing. He was taking his task very, *very* seriously.

At last, Justin turned to face his family and explain what he had learned on his mission. "As you can see, the right side of the take-out menu lists the specials, like the Fangs-giving Turkey Plate." He pointed to one of his notes, then pointed to another, "And the Count of Monte Cristo Sandwich on 'garlic-style' bread."

As her son spoke, Mrs. Russo examined one of the take-out menus that he'd plucked from the trash outside the Late Nite Bite at Juliet's suggestion. "Justin, isn't this all stuff from the menu?" she asked. "Why did you write it on the whiteboard?"

"It was a spy mission," Justin explained patiently. "I'm debriefing you. Without the board, we'd just be sitting around looking at menus." His mom clearly had no idea how a proper spy meeting went.

Suddenly, Mr. Russo's eyes grew wide. "Hold up." He eagerly scanned Justin's notes. "'Garlic-style'— Open all night— Count— Fangs! They're vampires!" he exclaimed.

"The Van Heusens are vampires?" Justin repeated. He didn't like the sound of that. They hadn't *seemed* like the blood-sucking type. Especially not Juliet.

"The people from the Late Nite Bite are vampires, and now the Van Heusens?" Max asked, getting confused. Then he got excited. "We're being overrun by vampires!"

Jumping up from the table, Max sent his chair clattering to the floor. "We've got a vampire war on our hands! *Hasta la vista*, baby!" he shouted, slipping into his Terminator voice. Then he ran for the door. "And that was the Terminator!" he yelled over his shoulder.

As soon as Max had left the restaurant, Alex sighed. "Okay, he's gone," she announced. "We should pack up and move." Immediately, she added silently.

But Mr. and Mrs. Russo had bigger things on their mind than Alex and Max's squabbles. Mr. Russo started to pace back and forth, deep in thought. "So they're vampires?" he asked. "That doesn't mean we can't beat them at their own game. They've got—what, a castle-dungeon theme? We've got a subway-station theme. So all we need to do is make people really feel like they're in a New York City subway station while they're here. Complete the experience for them."

"I'll just write that on the whiteboard to make it official," Justin said, his pen raised.

"Oh, I get it!" Mrs. Russo said brightly as she caught on to her husband's plan. "We can move the turnstile by the bathrooms over to the front door! Create a line out the front door to make the place look really busy, like those discotheques do!"

Alex raised an eyebrow. "Discotheques?" she repeated, shaking her head. "This could be the worst family meeting ever."

"No, no!" Mr. Russo said excitedly. "It's coming together! Late Nite Bite, you don't know what bear you just poked. *Grrrrrowl!* I'm the bear!"

Mr. and Mrs. Russo began to unscrew the turnstile so that they could move it outside the front door. While his parents were distracted, Justin grabbed Alex and pulled her into a corner.

"I need to talk to you," he said in a low voice. "I've got a date with Juliet Van Heusen. I need your help sneaking around Mom and Dad."

Alex raised an eyebrow. Sneaking around Mr. and Mrs. Russo was something Alex had experience with—a *lot* of experience.

Justin, on the other hand? Not so much. "Well, you came to the right place," she replied. "You definitely don't want to get caught dating the competition."

"What do I do?" Justin asked.

Alex's answer was simple and direct. "Use magic," she said. Her brown eyes sparkled, as they always did when she was coming up with a plan to get around her parents' rules.

"That's it?" Justin said, disappointed. He was expecting something a little more complicated from his sister, especially considering her years of experience sneaking around and breaking rules.

"Would you have thought of it?" asked Alex.

"No," Justin admitted.

"Okay, then," Alex said. "If there's nothing else you need, I've got to get started on my plan for getting Max and those annoying impressions out of the house for the summer."

As Alex walked over to the door, she did a quick impression of Max as the Terminator. "I'll be back!" Then she slipped back into her regular voice. "No, you won't, Max! No, you won't."

The next night, when it was time for the dinner rush, the Russos were ready. The shiny subway turnstile had been moved just outside the restaurant, where it gleamed in the light of the setting sun. In the subway car, a crowd had gathered. A very hungry crowd.

As part of their renovation, Mr. and Mrs. Russo had set everything up so that the customers would experience a fake subway ride before they entered the dining room. Overhead, the lights of the subway car flickered on and off, just as they did during a real ride on the subway. A recording of subway train noises played on repeat.

Mr. Russo's voice boomed over the speakers.

"Waverly Sub Station," he announced. "Next stop, Delicious!"

As the doors to the dining room *whooshed* open, an impatient customer demanded, "Can we eat now?"

"Not yet, sir," Mr. Russo replied. "First, we have a little subway entertainment!" He pointed to Alex's best friend, Harper Evans, and whispered loudly, "Harper, you're on!"

With her unique fashion sense and her wardrobe of one-of-a-kind handmade clothes, Harper usually didn't mind being the center of attention. And as one of the few normal people who knew about the Russo kids' magical abilities, Harper also knew that she was a trusted friend of the Russo family. But pretending to be a drum-playing subway musician in the middle of the Waverly Sub Station? That seemed a little extreme, even for Harper.

"You know, I've been thinking, Mr. Russo," Harper began as she flicked her long, light brown hair over her shoulders. "I'm not a trained monkey. I wouldn't do ballet for my mom's bridge club, and I wouldn't play violin for my dad's poker buddies, and I won't do this for you."

Mr. Russo eyed Harper. He knew how to get around this stubborn streak. "You look nice today, Harper," he said sincerely.

It worked. Harper grinned as she grabbed a pair of drumsticks. "Two, three, four!" she counted off the beat as she began to bang on three plastic buckets and a garbage-can lid.

The noise was deafening in the small restaurant. Two customers made a face and moved to leave—until Max stepped in front of them.

"Hello, New Yorkers," he said, trying out a new impression: Jerry Seinfeld. "It's me, Jerry Seinfeld, at Waverly Sub Station. I love sandwiches. Why do they call them sandwiches? There's no sand in them. They're not made by witches. What's the deal?"

As Max took a bow, a few customers took the opportunity to slip past him and leave the restaurant.

"Please, I just want coffee," a customer said with a sigh.

"I'll get it," Alex volunteered. Then she leaned close to Max. If he kept doing those impressions . . . "You'll get it soon!" she hissed in warning.

As a customer sat down at the counter, Mrs. Russo walked over to take his order. "So, do you want to try one of our new Grand Central Grinders or not?" she asked.

"I'm not sure," replied the customer. "What's in it?"

"I don't know," Mrs. Russo said. "My husband changed the menu to all subway names. Just eat it!"

"Wow, you're really rude," the customer said in shock.

"Yeah, just like the people in the subway,"

Mrs. Russo retorted. "Welcome to the theme!"

As Mrs. Russo left for the kitchen, Alex returned with the coffeepot. Justin came up next to her.

"So, Romeo, did you figure out how you're using magic to date Juliet?" Alex asked him in a low voice.

"I added five minutes to the break schedule by using an Orb of Spirit Confusion," Justin said proudly. "Now I'll be able to date her for twenty-five minutes at a time!"

"You used an Orb of Spirit Confusion to do this?" Alex asked in disbelief. "You could have used the Orb to stop time, freeze Mom and Dad so they can't find you, create an alternate reality where you and Juliet can date for a whole year, but it's only, like, a minute of time here. Something *big* and *magical!*"

Justin grinned. "I also used it to grow two inches!" he bragged.

Alex sighed. "You are a wiz-idiot."

"Hey, you use magic your way, and I'll use magic mine," Justin snapped.

"Fine, I will!" Alex announced. She pulled her wand out of her back pocket and waved it at Justin. "There, now you're two inches shorter, just like you used to be!"

Harper, who'd just finished her plastic-bucket drum solo, walked over. "What's up, shorty?" she asked Justin.

Justin shook his head. He could deal with Alex and Harper for one more hour. After all, it was only one more hour until his break.

And that meant only one more hour until his first date with Juliet. Justin could hardly wait!

Chapter Four

Later that afternoon, Justin was in the middle of the most amazing date of his life. Things with Juliet couldn't have gone better. Now they were walking down the sidewalk, their arms linked. They stopped to buy some roasted chestnuts from a street vendor.

"And that is the definition of the word *definition*," Justin finished his lengthy story with a joke. He hoped that Juliet would get it.

And from the sound of her beautiful laugh, she did! "Hey, what's the definition of the word *word*?" she asked.

Justin grinned. Without a doubt, Juliet was the most fantastic girl he'd ever met. "Where have you been all my life?" he asked.

"If I told you, you wouldn't believe me," Juliet replied, glancing at the sidewalk.

Justin knew what it was like to have a secret you felt you couldn't share. It hurt. And he didn't want to see Juliet in pain. Ever. "Juliet," he said, "I know you're a vampire."

Juliet looked surprised. Then she smiled. "Okay, then maybe you will believe me," she said. "And while we're on it, I know you're a wizard. I could tell because of your scent."

Justin's face grew red. "Sorry. I've been slicing ham," he tried to explain.

But Juliet shook her head. "I'm talking about your wizard scent—part brick, part pine needles," she continued. "Vampires have a strong sense of smell—stronger than werewolves, really. But people don't want to get past the fangs and the blood-drinking to learn the specifics."

"You don't seem like other vampires I know," Justin said.

"That's because my parents wanted me to fit in better and gave me a soul," Juliet confided to Justin. "I have feelings."

"And what do your feelings tell you?" asked Justin.

Juliet's smile grew wider. "That we need to do this again," she replied.

"But your parents don't like me," Justin pointed out. "And my parents wouldn't like it if they knew I was going out with a competitor's daughter."

"I'm sorry," Juliet said softly. Then her voice grew stronger. "But I don't care what Daddy has to say about it. I'm going to tell him and Mother about you!"

"You know what?" Justin said, encouraged by her determination. "I'm going to tell my parents, too. Then maybe we can have a date that lasts longer than my twenty-five-minute break from work!"

"It was fun," Juliet agreed. "I've never gone to a movie just to see the coming attractions before."

"The fun part was you," Justin replied as they approached the Waverly Sub Station. "I don't want to say good-bye."

"Neither do I. Let's just count to three and turn and walk away," Juliet suggested.

"You said, 'Count'!" Justin cried, cracking up. "Get it? You're a vampire . . . Count Dracula . . ."

But Juliet wasn't smiling. "Yeah," she said. "We don't do Dracula jokes."

"Sorry," Justin quickly apologized. "Okay, I've got to go. I'd hug you, but I don't want to get my wizard scent on you before you tell your parents. How about I give you a mind hug instead?"

"Okay," Juliet said. "I'll give you one, too."

Justin and Juliet stared at each other for a long moment.

"Ahhh," Justin said at last. "That's nice."

Alex, who had been keeping an eye out from the doorway of the restaurant, cleared her throat loudly. "Romeo. Juliet. Let's wrap it up with the looky-looks," she called.

Juliet turned around to look at her. "Oh, hey, Oprah!" she said cheerfully.

"That's not Oprah," Justin corrected her. "That's Alex."

Juliet shook her head. "No, that's Oprah. She comes in and orders the Nosfera-Tuna."

Alex shrugged and smiled. "It's hilarious when the sandwich is ready and they call out, 'Oprah!' and everybody looks to see it's just me. I mean, that is *never* not funny." She gave Juliet a little wave as she turned and walked into the Waverly Sub Station.

Justin gave Juliet one last smile before he followed Alex. There were a few more customers in the restaurant, though it was just as loud and annoying as it had been before Justin left on his date.

Max was working the cash register. He bent his pinky finger and held it up to his mouth in an impression of Dr. Evil from the Austin Powers movies. "That'll be six-fifty out of . . . one *miiiiiiillion* dollars!"

The customer said something in response, but no one could hear him with Harper banging on the plastic buckets and garbage lid.

"Harper, you're getting really good at that!" Mrs. Russo yelled over the noise.

"I am?" Harper asked, surprised.

"No. Of course not," Mrs. Russo replied. "This whole subway theme is stupid."

Harper didn't need to take that. She was an artist! She threw down her drumsticks and stormed out of the restaurant. In the sudden silence, Justin decided to make his announcement.

"Mom, Dad, I've got to talk to you about the Van Heusens," he said.

Mr. Russo looked up from his order pad. "Have you found a way to destroy them and send them into the bowels of the Earth?" he asked hopefully.

Justin gulped. This was not starting well. "No, actually," he replied. "Not all the Van Heusens are evil."

Mrs. Russo raised an eyebrow. "They've stolen all our business and forced us into this subway nonsense," she replied. "I've hated this subway car since I heard someone at an auction say, 'Sold. To the guy eating a sandwich.'"

"It was a great deal!" Mr. Russo protested. "They included towing!"

"The Van Heusens are evil," Mrs. Russo

continued firmly. "And so is anyone who is related to them, friends with them, or eats in their restaurant."

There was a long pause.

Then Mrs. Russo said, in a much friendlier tone of voice, "Now, what did you want to tell us, honey?"

Justin's mouth suddenly felt very dry. What *did* he want to say? "Uh . . . uh . . . the average room temperature of an igloo is sixty-one degrees Fahrenheit when people are in it," he stammered.

"That's nice, sweetie," Mrs. Russo replied. "Maybe someday you can grow up, buy an igloo at an auction, and build a whole restaurant around it, like your father."

"I am an entrepreneur!" Mr. Russo protested.

Alex grabbed Justin's arm and pulled him aside. "Look, you can't come clean about Juliet," she said urgently. "When they find out, there's going to be chaos. And that's the chaos

I'm going to need to cover up my plan to send Max away for the summer." So we don't have to listen to all those dumb impressions, she added silently. Then, out loud, she finished, "There's a magical underwater sea-horse ranch that's all filled up, but I've got him slowly moving up the wait list."

Suddenly, the door flew open and Juliet rushed into the restaurant.

"Justin! I told my parents!" she exclaimed.

"Wow, that was quick," Justin replied.

"Well, it didn't take long to say, 'I like Justin.' And for them to say, 'Whaaa?!?!' How did your parents take it?" she asked.

"Um . . . yeah. I'm going to need another day with it," Justin said.

"I don't think you're going to have another day," Juliet said. "You might have another five seconds to squeeze it in."

"What do you mean?" Justin asked, puzzled.

But Juliet didn't have a chance to answer him. At that moment, Mr. and Mrs. Van Heusen stormed into the Waverly Sub Station!

"We've come to reclaim our daughter!" Mr. Van Heusen bellowed.

"Yeah!" added Mrs. Van Heusen.

Mr. Russo stood up. "Who are you?" he asked.

"Alucard Van Heusen," Mr. Van Heusen said, introducing himself. "And this is my wife, Cindy."

"Juliet, get away from that boy," Mrs. Van Heusen ordered.

"Of all the sneaky tricks to use!" Mr. Van Heusen spat. "Sending your boy over to play with my Juliet's affections—that is low, even for a wizard."

Mrs. Russo wasn't about to stand by and let anyone insult her family. "Like six-feet-in-the-ground low? Eh, vampires?" she asked in an icy voice.

42

Mr. Russo turned to his wife. "You may want to stay out of this," he cautioned her.

"Your husband is right," Mrs. Van Heusen said to Mrs. Russo. "You've unleashed the wrath of Alucard." Then she lowered her voice as she leaned closer to Mrs. Russo. "Please pretend you're scared, or I'll have to hear about it all night."

"Prepare to meet your doom!" Mr. Van Heusen shouted, getting into the spirit of things. Then he noticed Alex. "Oh, look— Oprah's here!"

"Hey, Al. Hi, Cindy," Alex said calmly.

Mrs. Van Heusan smiled at Alex. Then, turning back to Mr. and Mrs. Russo, she frowned. "Let's cut to it," Mrs. Van Heusen said. "Your son needs to stay away from our daughter. She doesn't know what she's doing. Her fangs haven't even come in yet."

Suddenly Mr. Russo understood what was going on. He turned to Justin, shocked.

"You're *dating* the competition? How could you do this to us? I might expect this from Alex—but you?"

Alex nodded. "Yeah, that's totally something I would do," she agreed.

"Dad, we really like each other," Justin said.

Ignoring his son's puppy-dog look, Mr. Russo spun around to face Mr. Van Heusen. "Oh, I get it," he said. "You sent your daughter over to make him fall in love as part of your sick plan to destroy us!"

"How would that destroy us?" Justin asked, confused.

"They're vampires!" Mr. Russo explained. "They're handsomer, smarter, and more cunning than we are. They're like shaved wolves that can vote!"

Juliet crossed the room to face her parents. "Daddy, Mother, the moments I've spent with Justin have been the best twenty-five minutes of my life!" she said, pleading.

"Well, those moments are over," Mr. Van Heusen said firmly. "Come on."

Poof!

In a blinding flash, Mr. and Mrs. Van Heusen transformed into bats and flapped around the restaurant. When they tried to leave, though, they flew right into the glass door.

Juliet sighed as she gave Justin a long, sad look. She opened the front door for her parents, who quickly flew off.

Then she followed them into the night.

Chapter Five

The next day, the Waverly Sub Station was open for business as usual. And the Russos were still doing their best to keep the new and improved subway theme as realistic as possible.

They were also doing their best to forget about the scene with the Van Heusens—and Justin's unfortunate crush.

In the middle of the restaurant, Max wore a spiky black wig and did a crazy dance. He stuck out his lower lip as far as he could. With a big flourish, he finished his dance and announced, "Mick Jagger. Thank you."

The customers nearby weren't impressed. They left without ordering anything to eat.

Across the restaurant, Mr. Russo poured a hot cup of coffee for a customer. The woman caught his eye. "Excuse me," she said loudly, trying to be heard over the screeching subway sound track that was blasting in the background. "Can you turn that sound down? I get it—it's a subway. But I just want my coffee."

Mr. Russo tried to smile patiently. "Look, we're selling the *experience* of being underground in a subway," he explained for the hundredth time. "*And* friendly, courteous service—so shut up and enjoy it!"

At the counter, Harper helped Mrs. Russo refill the napkin holders. She was deep in thoughts—of the Justin variety. It was no secret that Harper had been in love with Justin practically since she had first met him. She was more upset about Justin's crush on Juliet than anyone.

"I know what you're thinking right now," Harper said to no one in particular. "You're thinking that I'm threatened by this new girl that's become a part of Justin's life. Well, I'm not! He likes to dabble with the exotic girls—the werewolves, the centaurs, the vampires. But Old Steady is going to win this race."

Next to her, Mrs. Russo smiled. "Good for you, Harper," she said encouragingly. Compared to Juliet Van Heusen, Harper would be a prize girlfriend for Justin!

"You want to know who Old Steady is?" Harper continued, happy to have an audience. She pointed to herself. "This girl!"

Nearby, Justin was oblivious to the conversation Harper was having with his mom. He was so depressed that he barely looked up as he talked to a customer sitting at the counter.

"The specials today are . . . What am I talking about?" Justin said sadly. "There's nothing special about today, tomorrow, or ever." He stared out the window longingly in the direction of the Late Nite Bite.

Alex shook her head as she watched her brother. It was pathetic, really. He got so easily swept up in love. With a sigh, she went over to talk to him. "You've got to get over your twenty-five-minute girlfriend," she said firmly.

"You know what I found out?" Justin said, ignoring Alex's remark. "I fall in love fast."

Alex stifled a laugh. That wasn't a shocking revelation.

"But you know what's different about it this time?" Justin continued. "When I'm not with her, my heart hurts."

Alex stared at Justin. This *was* shocking. Maybe she shouldn't be quite so hard on her big brother. "You know what?" she said. "I believe you. Usually you whine for a half hour, and then I wave an action figure in front of you and you're fine."

"Not this time," Justin replied sadly.

"Oh, for the love of cheese!" Alex exclaimed as she rolled her eyes. "Come with me."

Alex grabbed Justin's arm and led him through the back of the restaurant to the kitchen. At one end of the kitchen was a heavy steel door. With a quick backward glance to make sure her parents weren't watching, Alex used all her strength to open the door and slip inside, dragging Justin behind her. Within a few seconds, Alex and Justin were inside the Wizard's Lair.

There were lots of strange places under-ground in New York City: Cramped studio apartments with no windows. Creepy, slimy sewers. Miles and miles of subway tunnels. But it's safe to say that there was nowhere in the whole city like the Russo family's Wizard's Lair. The sprawling, brick-walled basement was filled with unique and fascinating magical artifacts, like the top-of-the-line Hocus-Focus crystal ball and the Insta-Tripper Piece o' Cake, an enchanted globe that could transport a wizard to anywhere in the world—instantly!

If Mr. and Mrs. Russo saw their kids going into the Wizard's Lair without permission, they would stop them immediately. And Alex didn't have time to follow their rules about only performing magic with adult supervision. The Justin situation was getting more serious by the minute. And, even worse, it was taking her away from an even more important project: sending Max to sleepaway camp for the whole summer so she could finally have a break from his awful impressions!

Alex crossed the room to a gargoyle that was all dressed up for Mardi Gras, complete with strands of shiny purple, green, and gold beads draped around its neck. She grabbed a pair of glasses off the gargoyle's face and held them out to Justin.

"Put these on," Alex ordered.

Justin, however, had been tricked by Alex before. Sure, they *looked* like ordinary glasses—but in the wizard world, you could never tell what kind of crazy spell had been placed on something. "Why?" he asked suspiciously.

"I'm going to help you," Alex said impatiently. She had thought it was pretty obvious.

"Why?" Justin repeated, sounding even more suspicious.

"Because your sadness grossed me out," Alex said, wrinkling her nose.

That was a good enough reason for Justin. He slipped the glasses onto his face.

Poof!

Justin was immediately transformed into a totally different-looking guy!

"Now you and Juliet can continue to date," Alex explained. "While you're wearing the glasses, everyone will see you as a completely different person."

When Justin stared in the mirror to get a glimpse of his new look, his regular reflection stared back at him—with the addition of the glasses, of course. But Alex, and anyone else who ran into him, could see that his outward appearance had changed. Justin took off the glasses and instantly turned back into his usual self.

"Those are just a loan," continued Alex. "I'm going to need them back at a moment's notice."

For the third time, Justin asked, "Why?"

"For my plan to get rid of Max!" Alex said brightly. "There's this guy coming over whose kid is number one on the wait list for sea-horse camp. He has to think I'm the camp director, because I'm kicking his kid off the wait list for pinning a starfish on a walrus and calling him the sheriff."

"That doesn't make any sense," Justin replied.

"That's why I need the glasses, dude!" Alex exclaimed. "If those words don't come out of a grown-up's mouth, we're stuck with Jerry 'The Terminator' Seinfeld all summer!"

Justin grinned at Alex as he put the glasses on again. Sure, her magic was strange, daring, and sometimes downright risky.

But this time, it might actually save the day!

Chapter Six

That night, eyeglasses firmly pressed up on his nose, Justin went on his second date with Juliet. His alternate appearance when wearing the glasses was so convincing that he dared to take her out to dinner right in front of her parents—at the Late Nite Bite!

Just like on their first date, Justin was having the most amazing time of his life. They sat across from each other in a booth against a wall covered with mirrors. Juliet was in the middle of telling Justin all about the Revolutionary War—which she had experienced firsthand.

"So there we are, yelling, 'The British are coming! The British are coming!'" she said, shaking her fists in the air.

"You were there? During the Revolutionary War?" Justin asked, impressed. "I thought it was just Paul Revere."

Juliet rolled her eyes. She had heard that before. "Oh, yeah, Paul 'Check me out over here' Revere. That guy was such an attention hog."

As Justin cracked up, he couldn't help but notice their reflection in the mirror. Actually, he noticed only one reflection: his own. Juliet had no reflection at all.

"Wow, it's true," Justin remarked. "Vampires don't show up in mirrors!"

"Yeah—doing our hair is total guesswork," Juliet replied with a laugh.

Across the room, the Van Heusens smiled as they watched Juliet laugh and have fun with her new friend.

"Look at Juliet with that new boy," Mrs. Van Heusen said approvingly. "They're so sweet together! Juliet really seems to be enjoying him."

"I knew we did the right thing, keeping her away from that Russo urchin," Mr. Van Heusen said, nodding. "And you know I could have unleashed my wrath on him anytime I wanted to."

"I know, sweetheart," Mrs. Van Heusen said as she patted her husband on the arm. "I know."

Suddenly, the door to the Late Nite Bite slammed open, and Alex rushed into the restaurant. She ran up to Justin. "It's time!" she said urgently. "Give me the glasses."

"Uh, I'm in the middle of something," Justin replied, looking around nervously.

"Sheriff boy's father is here!" Alex argued. "It's now or never."

Before Justin even knew what she was doing, Alex grabbed the glasses off his face.

Poof!

Justin's appearance was instantly transformed! Once again, he looked like his usual self.

Justin had to do something—and fast. He quickly slouched low in the corner of the booth and opened a big menu in front of his face. But it was too late. The Van Heusens had already recognized him.

"Justin Russo!" Mrs. Van Heusen cried. "A wizard trick!"

Alex's eyes grew wide. Oops! "Good luck, you two," she said quickly. "I'm rooting for you!" Then she dashed out of the restaurant, the magic glasses held tightly in her hand.

Mr. Van Heusen stood up straight and tried to look as threatening as possible. "Juliet, get away from him!" he ordered at the top of his voice. "We forbade you to see him!"

Justin stood up to face Mr. Van Heusen. "I'm sorry, sir," he began. "But I would never do anything to hurt your daughter or your business."

"We thought she was with a nice boy from school!" Mrs. Van Heusen said.

"He *is* a nice boy!" Juliet spoke up. "That's what I've been trying to tell you. There's no difference between the boy you saw and Justin. Why can't you just let us be happy?"

Mr. and Mrs. Van Heusen were quiet for a moment. Justin seized the opportunity to make his case. It was now or never. "With all due respect, Mr. and Mrs. Van Heusen, this restaurant feud is between you and my parents," he said. "Juliet and I have nothing to do with it! Please let us be together. I really care about Juliet."

Justin's words touched Mrs. Van Heusen's

heart—or they would have, if she'd had a heart. Even more importantly, they reminded her of when she'd fallen for Mr. Van Heusen, such a long time ago. With a smile, she turned to her husband. "Come on, Alucard," she said gently. "You're an old romantic softy. Remember when we were young and in love a thousand years ago?"

Mr. Van Heusen smiled at the memory. "It seems like just yesterday we were drinking King Arthur," he replied.

Justin wrinkled up his face. "Is that a brand of soda?" he asked nervously.

"Uh, yeah. Sure, kid," Mr. Van Heusen stammered.

Mrs. Van Heusen beamed at Justin. "You can see Juliet as often as you want," she said.

"But remember," warned Mr. Van Heusen, "I am capable of unleashing my wrath . . . as long as I'm not distracted." He spun around to yell at a customer. "Hey! It's not unlimited sauces! You get *one*." Could nobody understand the meaning of portion control?

"Way to unleash that wrath, dear," Mrs. Van Heusen said sarcastically.

Justin couldn't stop grinning as he reached for Juliet's hand. "You've inspired me, Mr. and Mrs. Van Heusen!" he announced. "I'm sure when my parents see how happy I am with Juliet, they'll be just as accepting as you are! Come on, Juliet—let's go tell them!"

Justin and Juliet left the Late Nite Bite and ran down the street to the Waverly Sub Station. When they burst in the door, Mr. and Mrs. Russo stood up. They took one look at their grinning faces and entwined hands and didn't even give Justin a chance to speak.

"Absolutely not!" Mr. Russo exclaimed. "What are you thinking? Those people are stealing our business!"

"We will not let you betray this family, Justin," Mrs. Russo added. "I don't care how happy you are! Well, as a mother, I care about your happiness. But as a restaurant owner, I don't."

Alex walked into the restaurant and sat in a booth to watch the fight.

"You know, Mr. and Mrs. Van Heusen were accepting, loving, and tolerant of us," Justin said angrily. "And they have no souls!"

"I could never have seen this coming," Mr. Russo said, shocked. "Alex, you are officially the good child in this family."

A look of horror crossed Alex's face. "'Good child?'" she repeated. "You're calling *me* the 'good child?' Think about it. What has Justin done wrong? He fell in love with somebody. Big deal. *I'm* the one who's been trying to get Max sent off to an undersea camp for the summer!"

Alex's words sunk through her father's haze of anger. "You're trying to get rid of your brother?" Mr. Russo asked with a frown.

"Yeah, but it didn't work out," sighed Alex. "The wizard kid's dad was a cop. He knew that there's no such thing as a walrus sheriff."

"I don't think you need to be a cop to know there's no walrus sheriff," Juliet pointed out.

"Look," Alex continued, ignoring the other girl's remark and turning her attention to her parents. "Justin should be allowed to go out with Juliet and you guys should be focused on punishing me for what I almost did to Max."

"She's right, Jerry," Mrs. Russo said to her husband. "Our feud with the Van Heusens has blinded us to something a little more important."

"Our son's happiness," Mr. Russo agreed. "Justin, Juliet, you guys can date."

"So it's official!" Juliet exclaimed happily.

"Not until I write it on the whiteboard!" Justin corrected her as he grabbed the dry-erase marker.

"Some people might find that weird, but I

find it charming," Juliet said, her voice filled with admiration.

Mr. Russo turned to Alex. "I see what you did here," he said knowingly. "You made a sacrifice for your brother. You really are the good one."

Alex started to squirm. "Dad, you're making me really uncomfortable," she complained.

"I know," Jerry said with a grin. "That's why I keep saying it. You're the good one. *You're* the good one. *You're* the *good* one!"

Alex clamped her hands over her ears. "Daddy, stop! Daddy, stop!" she yelled. This was worse than nails on a chalkboard. Worse than a summer of Max. Worse than . . .

Just then, Max walked into the room to see Justin and Juliet hugging, and Alex chanting "Stop!" at the top of her lungs. "What's going on?" he asked.

"Alex almost sent you away to an undersea

camp where everyone rides sea horses," Justin told him.

Max's mouth dropped open. His eyes shone with delight. "Oh, my gosh!" he yelled. "I would love that!"

He ran over to Alex and threw his arms around her, giving her the biggest hug he could. "You're so great, Alex! You're a great sister. I'm going to work all summer to do an impression of you!" Max exclaimed

A look of panic crossed Alex's face. Okay, she had been wrong. Being good was better than this. Much better.

"Max, please," she said. "I'm begging you not to do that."

But Max had already begun. "Max, please. I'm begging you not to do that," he repeated in his best impression of Alex.

"Please leave me alone!" Alex pleaded.

"Please leave me alone!" repeated Max.

"Stop," ordered Alex.

"Stop," Max mimicked her.

Alex sighed deeply and buried her face in her hands so that she couldn't see Max copy her every move. This was the absolute last time she did something good for *either* of her brothers.

No matter what!

PART
TWO

Chapter One

It was a relatively quiet Saturday night in New York City. The streets weren't packed. The subways were running smoothly, and the Waverly Sub Station was closed for the night. But the loft above the sub shop, where the Russo family lived, was a flurry of activity. In the kitchen, Mrs. Russo was putting the finishing touches on an elaborate dinner that she'd cooked from scratch. Mr. Russo was carefully setting the table with a fancy tablecloth and the family's nicest dishes and silverware. Justin Russo walked into the spacious living room, carrying a candelabra.

"Okay, Juliet's going to be here any minute," Justin said nervously, pulling at his suit. "How do I look? Do you think the boutonniere is too over-the-top? What about this candelabra?"

"It would be fine, if you had a hunchback and a bell tower," his father joked. "Justin, relax. This is going to be fine."

"It's just that this is the first meal Juliet is having with our family, and I don't want anything to go wrong," Justin explained.

He had good reason to be worried. Justin's relationship with Juliet Van Heusen had gotten off to a rocky start. It wasn't her fault that her parents had opened up a competing sandwich shop called the Late Nite Bite just down the street from the Russo family restaurant, the Waverly Sub Station. And it wasn't her fault that she was a vampire. And it most definitely wasn't *Justin's* fault that he was a wizard. That was totally his dad's fault. But still, Mr. and Mrs. Russo had forbidden Justin to date her . . . until, after a lot of begging, they'd finally changed their minds.

Justin liked Juliet more than any girl he'd ever met, and now that he finally had permission to date her, he didn't want his wacky family to do anything that might make Juliet change her mind about dating him.

"Sweetie, what could possibly go wrong?" Mrs. Russo called from the kitchen.

Just then, Alex and Max thundered down the stairs. "I think tonight might be the night I try to eat my dinner blindfolded," Max said.

"But then you won't know what you are eating," Alex started to say. But that gave her an idea for an awesome prank, so she quickly changed her tactic. "I mean, that's a great idea! You should totally do it!"

Then Alex noticed the fancy tablecloth. "Hey, what's with the tablecloth?" she asked her dad. "Did someone carve another dirty picture into the table?"

"It wasn't me," Max spoke up. Then he paused. "Wait, which dirty picture are we talking about?"

Mrs. Russo raised her eyebrows. "Good luck not being ashamed of us, sweetie," she said to Justin with a smile. Then she turned to Alex and Max. "Justin's new vampire girlfriend is coming over for dinner. I still can't get used to saying that."

"I can!" Mr. Russo sang out with a grin. "Justin's got a girlfriend! A vampire girlfriend! Justin's got a girlfriend!" Finishing his impromptu song, Mr. Russo laughed and elbowed his son in the ribs. Then he gave him a wink.

"Dad!" Justin said at once. Why did he have to be so uncool?

"Sorry," Mr. Russo apologized. "I'm just trying to get out all of my inappropriate behavior before she gets here. Hey, who wants to see my appendix scar?"

Ding-dong!

Justin sighed. Saved by the bell. His face grew even more serious. "That's her. Dad, I'm not opening the door until you put your shirt down," he said in a stern voice.

Mr. Russo shrugged. He thought scars would be a great icebreaker. Still, he tucked his shirt back in. As soon as the coast was clear, Justin opened the door. Juliet was standing there, looking especially pretty. "Hi, Justin," she said with a little wave.

"Hello, Juliet," Justin replied. "Why, you're a vision of loveliness and enchantment!"

Juliet smiled at him. "You're so cute when you give old-timey compliments." She giggled.

"Well, you're a vampire," Justin said as he led her into the living room. "Vampires are really old, right? I mean, not that you look old. You look great for your age! Which would be . . ."

But Juliet just shook her head. She knew exactly what Justin was up to. "Justin, I told you that I'm not telling you my age," she said. "If I did, you'd freak out. Like Caesar did. Oh, shoot!" She couldn't believe that she'd slipped up and given Justin a clue about how old she really was!

"I'm narrowing it down," Justin said, giving Juliet his most charming smile.

"Nobody cares!" Alex butted in, mimicking Justin's tone of voice.

Justin turned to gesture to his family. "Juliet, you know my family," he said.

"Hi, everybody. Wow, it smells great in here!" she exclaimed.

Mrs. Russo smiled broadly. She loved a

compliment. "I've prepared a special meal in honor of our special guest. I call it my Ten-Cheese Enchilada Surprise."

"The surprise is an eleventh cheese!" Max said hungrily, rubbing his stomach.

"Eleven cheeses in *one* dish?" Juliet asked, her eyes wide. "I'm sorry, Mr. and Mrs. Russo, but I don't think I can eat that."

"What do you mean?" asked Mrs. Russo, puzzled. "Just try it. You'll love them! It's really funny when Jerry eats them too fast and the spices make his forehead sweat."

Juliet looked uncomfortable. "I probably should have mentioned this earlier, but vampires are kind of health-conscious," she explained.

"Oh, so are we," Mrs. Russo said. "We stopped letting the kids drink soda for breakfast."

"Yeah, and our Chocolate Surprise Cake has raspberry jam in the middle," added Mr. Russo. "That's a fruit!" He held up a cake plate to reveal a giant chocolate cake, dripping with chocolate frosting and chocolate-covered raspberries.

"My surprise is that I don't floss so I can taste dinner in my dreams!" Max announced.

Juliet looked uncomfortable as she stared from the cake to Max's mouth and then back to the cake. "I'm really sorry, Mr. and Mrs. Russo," she said in a quiet voice.

"No, it's okay," Mr. Russo reassured her. "We've had him tested, and it's not what you think."

Mrs. Russo rolled her eyes. Her husband had missed the point—again. "She's talking about the *food*, Jerry," she said. "Juliet, you're right. This cheesy and chocolaty food could be considered unhealthy. And my family deserves better than that."

Mrs. Russo picked up the heavy casserole dish filled with Ten-Cheese Enchilada Surprise and dropped it in the garbage. Alex, Max, and

Mr. Russo gasped in horror. Had their mom gone mad?

Apparently, she had. "From now on, the Russos are going to eat much healthier," Mrs. Russo declared. "Isn't that right, Jerry?"

"Get in there, Dad!" pleaded Alex. "Fight for our cake!"

But Mr. Russo knew he was trapped. He smiled weakly at his wife. "Sure, honey," he said. "You know I always support your unpredictable whims."

"Thank you," Mrs. Russo replied. "Now throw that cake away."

As he whispered, "Sorry!" to Alex, Mr. Russo carried the Chocolate Surprise Cake over to the trash can. It took every ounce of willpower he had to dump it on top of the enchiladas.

"Wow, Juliet," Justin said, smiling sappily. "You've only been here for a few minutes, and my family is already better off for knowing you. You're incredible."

"No, you're the incredible one, Justin," Juliet said.

"Butterfly kiss!" Justin said in a cutesy voice.

As Justin and Juliet leaned in close to share a butterfly kiss, Alex made a face. "Well, there goes my appetite," she announced. "I guess this worked out after all."

Chapter Two

The next day, Alex was hanging out in the Waverly Sub Station with her best friend, Harper Evans, when Mrs. Russo dragged a giant garbage bag down the stairs from the loft. The two girls eyed her curiously. What was going on?

"Thanks to Juliet, I've seen the error of our ways," Mrs. Russo declared. "We're throwing out all this junk food, and we're never looking back!"

A look of panic crossed Alex's face as she leaped off her chair. "Wait, Mom!" she cried. "You can't do this!"

Mrs. Russo grinned. "Oh, honey," she said sweetly, "I'm your parent! I can do whatever I want."

"Well, then, I'm out," Alex retorted as she crossed her arms. "I was *this* close to eating meals with you guys out of convenience, but you just put a stop to that. Thanks for ruining our family!"

Alex dramatically stormed up the stairs to the loft, but when she reached the top, she seemed to have a change of heart. Turning around, she called out, "I'm just kidding. But seriously, I'm not eating with you guys." With that said, she entered the loft and closed the door firmly behind her.

Mrs. Russo shook her head as she opened the front door to take the trash out to the street. She nearly ran into Juliet, who was about to enter the restaurant.

"Oh, hey, Mrs. Russo!" Juliet said. She held open the door as Mrs. Russo struggled with the bulging garbage bag.

"Hi, Juliet," replied Mrs. Russo. "Guess what's in the bag?"

"Nothing but junk food," Juliet said, wrinkling her nose. "I smelled it from a mile away—vampire sense of smell and all. Hey, is Justin around?" Juliet sniffed the air. "Oh, he's upstairs."

Juliet walked toward the stairs, but before she could reach them, Harper blocked her path. Harper had had a crush on Justin for as long as she could remember. She wasn't happy that he had a new girlfriend and figured she should at least let Juliet know the situation.

"Well, look at you," Harper said slowly. "Cloudy day, so you're out without an umbrella."

"Excuse me?" Juliet asked.

"I know you're a vampire," Harper replied. "I'm Harper. And I just wanted to tell you that there's no hard feelings."

"Hard feelings?" repeated Juliet, who was thoroughly confused. "About what?"

"Oh, Justin didn't tell you?" Harper asked innocently. "That's just like him, always trying to spare other people's feelings. He and I have had an on-and-off relationship for years. We're off now, which is why you guys are on. So I'm cool."

As she spoke, she smiled at Juliet and unzipped her jacket.

Juliet leaped back as if she had been stung by a bee. "Why do you have garlic around your neck?" she exclaimed.

"Sorry," Harper said with a shrug. "I wasn't sure how this was going to go." She quickly zipped up her jacket to cover the garlic pendant.

"Oh, so you went out and made a garlic necklace," Juliet said angrily.

Harper felt her cheeks grow warm. "No, actually I had it," Harper explained. "It's for this pasta outfit that I'm working on."

A smile suddenly crossed Juliet's face as she realized who Harper was. "Oh, you're the food-for-clothes girl!" she said. "Justin has talked about you!" Juliet quickly asked, "Nice to meet you," and then headed upstairs.

Harper watched as Juliet went to spend time with Justin. Yeah, she said to herself. That's me, the food-for-clothes girl. Too bad Mrs. Russo just threw out all that junk food—I could have had a whole new wardrobe!

Chapter Three

Mrs. Russo's plans for serving healthy food to the whole family went way beyond tossing the junk food. Later that day, she proudly brought Mr. Russo and Max onto the terrace to show them her latest project—a rectangle of freshly hoed dirt.

"This is our new garden, where we will grow all sorts of exciting vegetables—including broccoli!" Mrs. Russo announced. "They say broccoli has near-magical qualities."

"It will be magical if I can get it down without a warm cheese sauce," Mr. Russo cracked.

Mrs. Russo glared at her husband, unamused. When she turned to walk back into the loft, Mr. Russo followed sheepisly behind her. Max, however, didn't move from the garden plot. "Hmm," he murmured aloud, lost in thought. "Magical qualities, eh?"

Mr. Russo stopped at the door. "Did you say something, Max?" he asked.

"Nope, didn't say a word!" Max replied. Then he whispered, "Magical qualities!"

Mrs. Russo leaned over to her husband. "Let's just pretend we didn't hear it that time," she suggested.

Mr. Russo nodded in agreement and followed her inside.

As soon as his parents were gone, Max took his wand out of his pocket. He pointed it at the garden and cast a spell: "Don't let this garden go to waste! Give all this food a lot more taste."

Poof!

A massive orange pumpkin appeared on the terrace!

Max's eyes widened. "Well, that was unexpected," he said.

It was safe to say that Max's spell hadn't gone *exactly* the way he had planned. The pumpkin was so big that it covered the entire garden plot. It had smashed the small table and chairs that the Russos used when they wanted to eat outside. There was only one thing for Max to do: act casual. He wandered into the living room, humming under his breath, and closed the curtains so no one would see what was growing outside.

Luckily, no one was paying much attention. Justin and Juliet had come upstairs and were— as usual—being all mushy. Alex watched, her stomach growing increasingly more upset.

"That Pilates class was great!" Justin said enthusiastically to Juliet. "I've never felt more physically or emotionally centered in all my life!"

"Are you ready to try yoga next?" Juliet asked him as she pulled her pretty blond hair into a ponytail.

Justin grew serious. "Okay, but there's something you should know about me that I don't want to come as a surprise," he began. "I have extremely hairy toes. If we're breaking up right now, just tell me."

Juliet smiled as she put her hand on Justin's arm. "I'll look past your hairy toes if you'll look past the fact that I'm already dead," she said.

While Justin and Juliet laughed, Alex rolled her eyes. As if the health-food kick wasn't annoying enough, now there were extreme amounts of exercise in the Russo loft!

"Would you care to join us, Alex?" Juliet asked. "Yoga will really help strengthen your core."

"No, thanks," Alex replied as she slouched in the corner of the couch. "I like my core loose and in front of the TV."

Just then, Mr. and Mrs. Russo entered the living room. They had both changed into workout gear: tight shirts, spandex shorts, and sneakers. Mrs. Russo looked pumped to start working out. Mr. Russo, on the other hand, looked slightly less enthusiastic.

Justin frowned. "Aren't those shorts a little tight, Dad?" he asked

"They're looser than I thought they'd be," Mr. Russo said.

Justin shrugged—his dad was an odd guy—and then he and Juliet left for their yoga class.

It was all too much for Alex. She was horrified. "Oh, my gosh!" she exclaimed. "*What* is going on here?"

"A total aerobic workout is what's going on!" Mrs. Russo replied. "It's the perfect complement to healthy eating."

Alex turned to her father "Dad? Are *you* okay with this?" she asked.

"Yes. Of course," Mr. Russo said—but he wasn't very convincing. "What's not to be okay with? It sounds like a great idea!"

As Mr. and Mrs. Russo started stretching, Alex turned away in disgust. "I gave up eating with you people, and now you're making it impossible for me to watch television in my own home. I'm so desperate, I'm thinking about going over to Harper's house!"

Then Alex noticed Max standing by the curtains. He was still humming and trying to act casual. Her eyes narrowed. "What are *you* doing?" she asked.

"Nothing," Max replied quickly—a little *too* quickly. "Why do you ask?"

"Because it looks like you're humming

suspiciously to try to look casual," Alex said.

"That's exactly what I was doing!" Max exclaimed.

Ah-ha! "Let's see what you're *really* up to!" Alex announced as she flung open the curtains.

There, gleaming in the sun, was the enormous pumpkin!

Mr. and Mrs. Russo had stopped stretching. "Max! What did you do?" his mother yelled when she saw the giant vegetable.

"I was just trying to use magic to make the vegetables taste better," Max tried to explain. "But instead, I've made a giant pumpkin. I'm going to live in it."

Alex nodded. "Curiously, I did not see that one coming," she said. "But it does make Max sense."

Max grabbed a spoon out of the kitchen. "First I need to carve a door in the side of it!" he said.

"Max. That's a spoon," Alex pointed out.

Max sighed and rolled his eyes at his sister. "I *know* what it's called, Alex," he replied. His sister could be so narrow-minded sometimes.

Alex shook her head as she grabbed her purse and got ready to leave. Two parents sweating through an aerobics routine in the living room. One brother on a vampire-inspired exercise kick. Another brother about to move into a giant pumpkin.

She had to get out of there!

Chapter Four

After storming out of the loft, Alex knew exactly where to go. She had problems to solve and only one place to find solutions.

Alex headed down the street to the Late Nite Bite, the restaurant that Juliet's parents owned. She hoped that no one there would be on some extreme exercise program she'd be forced to watch—and she hoped that no one there would nag her to eat healthy food. She was starving!

As she walked into the restaurant, Alex was surprised to see Harper sitting in one of the booths, eating a sandwich. "Harper, what are you doing here?" she asked.

"I'm waiting for Juliet so I can talk to her," Harper explained.

"I thought you already talked to her," Alex replied.

Harper nodded. "I did. But I panicked and told her that Justin and I were once in a relationship."

"You weren't," Alex pointed out.

"I know!" Harper exclaimed. "That's the problem. I lied."

Alex smiled. Typical Harper.

Her stomach practically roaring, Alex walked over to the counter. Harper quickly finished her sandwich and followed her.

Ding! Alex rang the bell. Suddenly, Juliet's father, Mr. Van Heusen, appeared.

"Alex Russo and friend, what a pleasant

surprise," he said smoothly. "What can I get for you?"

"Your daughter out of my house," Alex said, getting right to her first order of business. "She has made it impossible for me to eat anything unhealthy. Do you sell doughnuts? Because I'd love a doughnut with a scoop of vanilla ice cream in the hole. That's what the hole is for, you know."

Mrs. Van Heusen overheard Alex as she joined her husband behind the counter. "Ice cream in the hole of a doughnut!" she exclaimed. "Why didn't you think of that, Alucard?"

"I *did* think of that!" Mr. Van Heusen said loudly. "Remember? I told you this morning!"

"You know what?" asked Mrs. Van Heusen. "You're constantly talking, so it's hard to pick out what's important."

Harper turned to Alex. "This is like being

at home if my parents were monsters," she said. "Oh, what am I saying? It's exactly like being at home!"

"You know, with all the time Juliet's been spending with your brother, we could use an extra hand around here," Mrs. Van Heusen said to Alex. "What would you say to a part-time job at the Late Nite Bite?"

"Hmmm," Alex said thoughtfully. "On the surface, that doesn't sound like something I would do. But it *would* get me out of Family Exercise Night."

"Look at you!" Mrs. Van Heusen said admiringly. "So clever and cunning. Sometimes we wish Juliet had more of that."

"Yes," agreed Mr. Van Heusen, "in a lot of ways, you're probably more like a vampire than she is."

"Thank you," Alex replied, taking their remarks as a compliment.

"So it's settled," Mrs. Van Heusen announced.

"You'll both start working here immediately."

"Me, too?" Harper asked. "Yes!" That would make it so much easier to apologize to Juliet. And keep an eye on Justin. Plus, maybe she'd get free sandwiches out of the deal.

Mrs. Van Heusen leaned closer to Alex and Harper. "You know, we find Juliet's health kicks slightly irritating, too," she said in a conspiratorial whisper.

"Really?" Alex asked. "I thought all vampires were health-conscious."

"No, it's mainly the younger generation," Mr. Van Heusen said. "If you can believe it, they sometimes even try to get humans to eat better so they'll have healthier blood to suck! They're very fanatical about it."

Alex began to nod and then stopped. "*What* did you just say?" she asked, looking worried.

"I said they're fanatical about it," repeated Mr. Van Heusen.

"No, before that," Alex said.

"I said it's mainly the younger generation," Mr. Van Heusen replied as he tried to dodge Alex's question.

But she wasn't going to give up. "Yes, but *after* that," Alex pressed.

Finally Mrs. Van Heusen stepped in. "I think she's talking about the part where you mentioned how younger vampires try to get humans healthier before drinking their blood," she said.

"That's the one," Alex said with a nod. "Excuse me." She spun around and ran toward the door—where she hit her head on a low-hanging pipe. "You've got to be kidding me!" Alex groaned as she grabbed her head. Then she hurried out the door.

"But her shift just started!" complained Mr. Van Heusen.

"I'll cover her," Harper said with a sigh. "I knew how this was going to go. I just didn't think it would happen so soon."

Back at the loft, unaware of any impending danger, Justin was on the terrace. He was standing next to the enormous pumpkin.

"Hey, Max," Justin called. "There's some mail here for you."

"Hold on," Max's muffled voice called out. But Max was nowhere to be seen.

Justin jumped out of the way as a sword plunged out of the pumpkin. It cut a rectangular-shaped hole in the side of the pumpkin. "This is my mail slot," Max announced through the hole.

"Yeah, I get it," Justin said with a sigh.

"I hope you're not jealous that I moved out of the house before you did," Max's voice said through the pumpkin. "Tell Mommy and Daddy that I said hi. Loser!"

"Okay, I'll tell them," Justin replied. He walked back into the loft, yelling, "Hey, Mom and Dad, the kid living in the jack-o'-lantern thinks *I'm* a loser!"

Just then, Alex rushed in through the front door. "Justin!" she cried. "Let's talk about Juliet!"

A dreamy smile crossed Justin's face. "I could talk about her all day!" he said. "Isn't she the greatest?"

Alex waved a hand in the air as if to say, "Yeah, yeah." "She's cute, and she's looking past your jungle toes, and we're all excited about it," she said. Then she dropped the bombshell. "*And* she wants to drink your blood."

"What are you talking about?" Justin asked.

"I got a job over at the Late Nite Bite, and while I was there I found out that young vampires like to feed on the healthiest human blood they can find," Alex explained.

"I can't believe it," Justin said slowly. "*You* got a *job*?"

"I know—weird, huh?" Alex agreed. Wait!

That was not the point she was trying to make! "I think Juliet is getting you healthy so she can drink your blood."

"Come on, Alex," Justin said condescendingly. "My girlfriend is not planning to drink my blood! Juliet is a vampire with a soul, so she has a conscience. That's why she volunteers at a blood bank on the weekends."

"Keep talking," Alex encouraged Justin. She figured if he rambled on long enough, he would figure out the truth about Juliet's interest in him eventually. "You're almost there."

"And I bet you think it's weird that she sometimes salivates uncontrollably when I'm wearing V-neck T-shirts, too," Justin went on.

Alex gave him a look. Surely not even Justin could be this dense!

Suddenly, Justin got it. His mouth dropped open as a look of shock and terror crossed his face. "Oh, my gosh," he said. "My girlfriend's going to suck my blood!"

"Look at that!" Alex said approvingly. "You stuck the landing."

Normally, she would have teased Justin about his taste in girlfriends. But one look at the shock and terror on his face convinced Alex to keep quiet.

For now, anyway . . .

Chapter Five

Later that night, Juliet found Justin hanging around outside the Waverly Sub Station. "Hey, Justin!" she said excitedly. "I just finished my homework. Want to do something?"

Justin spun around, looking terrified. A thick wool scarf was wrapped around his neck. "Juliet!" he exclaimed. Then he tried to run away.

But he didn't get very far. Juliet was suddenly right in front of him.

"Vampire speed," Justin said to himself. "I forgot about that."

"Why are you wearing a scarf?" Juliet asked. "It's seventy-five degrees out."

"I'm not wearing a scarf!" Justin lied as he nervously wrapped the scarf tighter around his neck. "Oh, you mean this? Okay. I'm wearing a scarf."

"Why are you acting so weird?" Juliet asked with a frown. "You probably have heatstroke. Let's get that scarf off."

Justin was frozen with fear as Juliet approached him and began to unwind the long scarf from around his neck. She pulled both ends of the scarf to draw Justin closer to her.

"Hey, this evening I woke up and my fangs had come in," Juliet said in a flirty voice. "Look!"

Juliet opened her pretty red lips to show

Justin two white fangs gleaming in the moonlight. It would have been romantic—except for the teeny, tiny fact that . . . Justin was afraid for his life!

"Stay back!" Justin shrieked as he completely lost his cool. "Keep your filthy fangs away from my perfect, succulent neck!"

Justin dug around in his pocket and yanked out a string of garlic cloves, which he shook in Juliet's face.

Juliet stepped back in horror. "Justin! What are you doing?" she cried.

"Trying to save my life," Justin replied coldly. "Alex told me you're just trying to get me eating healthy so you can drink my blood."

"What?" Juliet exclaimed. "You're my boyfriend. I would *never* do something like that! Besides, aren't you always saying that your sister is up to no good? Why would you believe her?"

"It's a complicated relationship I have with

her," Justin said defensively. Then he saw how hurt Juliet looked and his tone changed. "I'm sorry, Juliet. I should have trusted you." Then his tone changed again. "But if you didn't want to suck my blood, why do you always salivate when I wear V-neck T-shirts?"

Juliet shrugged. "Because I like the way you look in V-neck T-shirts," she replied.

"I knew it!" Justin said to himself. Then he focused back on Juliet. "Look, I should've known better than to listen to Alex. I mean, just because she's working for your parents, she thinks she's an expert on vampires or something."

"She's working for my parents?" Juliet asked, sounding alarmed.

"Yeah, she's over there with Harper right now," Justin said.

"Oh, my gosh!" Juliet cried. "Justin, there's no easy way to say this, so I'm just going to come right out with it."

"Okay," Justin said with a grin. He was sure he knew what Juliet was about to say.

Juliet looked Justin straight in the eye. "My parents might be planning to drink their blood," she said.

"I love you, too!" Justin replied in a dreamy voice. Then he heard what Juliet had actually said. Oops! "Oh, wait. You didn't say what I thought you were going to say."

But Juliet wasn't paying attention. "Come on!" she said, grabbing his arm and pulling him into the sub shop. "Let's tell your parents!"

Juliet dragged Justin through the restaurant and into the loft, where Mr. Russo was picking at his food—although he wasn't quite sure it *was* food. He speared a white chunk with his fork. "What is this?" Mr. Russo asked.

"It's called jicama, Jerry," Mrs. Russo replied. "It's a white-fleshed edible tuber."

Mr. Russo wrinkled his nose. "I try not

to eat anything that sounds like something people should have removed," he said. Then, bravely, he took a bite. "Are you kidding me? This tastes like nothing. It's a waste of chewing time!"

"Mom! Dad!" Justin interrupted. "Juliet said she loved me. Well, she didn't, but I thought she was going to."

"Justin. Blood drinking," Juliet said tensely, trying to get him to focus.

"And she didn't freak out when I said it," Justin continued.

"Aww!" Mrs. Russo said, smiling.

"Thanks, Mom!" Justin replied.

"Alex. Harper. Danger!" Juliet said loudly.

"What?" Justin asked. "This is an important milestone for us."

Juliet decided that she had to take control of the situation. "My parents are about to drink Harper and Alex's blood!" she announced.

Mr. and Mrs. Russo gasped in horror.

"Okay, now that they know that, can we talk about us?" Justin asked, still not getting the urgency of the situation.

"Come on!" cried Juliet as she grabbed Justin's hand and ran out the door, back to the Late Nite Bite.

As Mr. and Mrs. Russo got up to leave, Max walked in from the terrace. He was covered with pumpkin guts from carving out his new home.

"Did the satellite guy come?" Max asked. "I've got to tell him where to put the dish."

"Max, we're in the middle of something here," Mrs. Russo replied in a rush. "Your sister and Harper are about to be bitten by vampires."

"Cool!" Max exclaimed. "That's better than satellite!"

"Come on, let's get over there," Mr. Russo said. Suddenly, he stopped. "Oh, my gosh. What if we can only save one? Alex is our daughter, but Harper has so much more potential."

"And we both know Harper would take care of us in our old age," Mrs. Russo pointed out. "We'll talk about it on the way."

Chapter Six

At the Late Nite Bite, the early dinner rush had just ended. The restaurant was empty except for Alex, Harper, and the Van Heusens.

Harper took advantage of the quiet to hang up an Employee of the Month sign with her name written on it. "It's only been six hours," she said, "but we know it's going to happen. I mean, the competition is me and her."

Harper pointed at Alex, who was slouched

in a booth pouring salt into a pepper shaker. "Salt always wins," Alex declared. "Pepper never sees it coming."

"All right, since it's between rushes, why don't we take your photos for your company IDs," Mr. Van Heusen suggested.

"There's only two employees," Alex replied.

"It's a state-law thing. Just take a picture," Mrs. Van Heusen snapped. "Sorry. I'm just a little hungry."

"Alex, you first," Mr. Van Heusen said, sounding a *little* calmer.

Alex crossed the restaurant and sat in a chair. Mr. Van Heusen pointed the camera at her.

"Okay, good," he said. "Just tilt your head a little. More. More. More."

Soon Alex's head was tilted so much that the side of her neck was completely exposed. "It's a little uncomfortable," she said with a frown.

"But it makes for a good picture," Mr. Van

Heusen assured her. "Chin out. Chin out. Really stretch it! Now, Cindy, why don't you get in there and help position her head?"

"But it's *Alex's* employee ID!" Harper spoke up.

"Oh, relax," Mr. Van Heusen said as he rolled his eyes. "Cindy's a vampire. She's not going to show up in the picture. Come on, Cindy."

But Mrs. Van Heusen paused. "I didn't know I was going first," she said. "I thought I was 'taking a picture' with Harper."

"I don't think we decided that," Mr. Van Heusen replied.

"No, we did," Mrs. Van Heusen argued. "You were going to 'take a picture' with Alex, who is a little more bitter."

"Would someone just take my picture?" Alex asked. "I'm cramping up over here."

"Fine!" Mrs. Van Heusen exclaimed as she gave up. She stood next to Alex, opened her mouth, and leaned in close to Alex's neck. . . .

Just then, Justin and Juliet burst into the room. "Alex! Harper!" yelled Justin.

"What are you guys doing here?" Alex asked, confused. "I'm in the middle of getting my company ID."

Meanwhile, Harper saw her chance. "Juliet, I kind of fibbed about me and Justin," she confessed. It felt so good to tell the truth.

"You know what? This can wait," Juliet told her.

"Why?" Harper asked.

"Because those vampires are going to suck your blood!" Justin said.

"What?" shrieked Alex as she jumped away from Mrs. Van Heusen.

"You're right—we *can* talk about this later," Harper said to Juliet.

"Cindy, is this true?" Alex asked.

"Well, kind of, yeah," admitted Mrs. Van Heusen. "But it's not so bad. It kind of feels like a mosquito bite. And then all your blood is gone."

"Dad, Mom, you said you'd stop doing this!" Juliet cried, her voice filled with disappointment. "Are we going to have to move again?"

"I know this embarrasses you, Juliet, but unfortunately, it's who we are," Mr. Van Heusen replied. "We're vampires. We can't all have the incredible self-control that you have."

"So you two were planning this the entire time?" Alex asked, shaking her head. "Unbelievable. Maybe this goes without saying, but I quit."

"I kind of need the job, so I'm going to take my chances," Harper said.

"You know what? I haven't eaten in the six months we've been here," Mr. Van Heusen announced. "And we all know the Jets aren't going anywhere in the playoffs, so I'm cool with drinking some blood and moving to Phoenix."

Mr. Van Heusen swooped toward Alex, baring his sharp fangs. As Justin and Juliet jumped up to try to save Alex, Mrs. Russo rushed into the room.

Bang!

And hit her head on the low pipe in the doorway!

"Mom!" Alex cried.

Then Mr. Russo rushed into the room.

Bang!

He, too, hit his head on the pipe.

"Dad!" cried Alex.

"Harper! We've come to save you!" Mrs. Russo yelled, rubbing her head.

"What about me?" Alex asked.

"You guys," Mr. Russo corrected his wife. "We've come to save *you guys.*"

Bang!

Max ran into the room, hitting his head on the pipe like everyone else in the family.

"Max!" Alex cried. She'd never thought

she'd be so happy to see her little brother.

And then he spoke, and the warm, fuzzy feelings went away.

"Did they bite her yet?" Max asked Justin urgently. "Did I miss it?"

Mr. and Mrs. Van Heusen took one look at Max, and they cowered, clinging to each other.

"Who is that boy?" demanded Mr. Van Heusen.

"Get him away from us!" Mrs. Van Heusen shrieked.

Alex seized the opportunity to escape while the Van Heusens moved as far away from Max as they could.

"What's going on?" Justin asked, confused. "It's like they're afraid of Max or something."

"It's not Max, it's his smell," Juliet replied, holding her nose.

"Believe it or not, this isn't even one of his worst days," Alex said.

"No, it's the pumpkin," Juliet explained.

"Vampires *hate* pumpkins—even more than garlic. That's why people originally put pumpkins outside their houses on Halloween—to keep away vampires."

"Oh, please, make it stop!" begged Mr. Van Heusen. "Just get that awful, awful boy away from us!"

"Not until you apologize for almost biting my daughter's neck and turning her into a vampire for all eternity," Mr. Russo demanded.

"All right, all right!" Mrs. Van Heusen said. "We're sorry. Maybe we can smooth this over with some ice cream."

"Really?" Mr. Russo asked. "You were just about to turn our daughter into a vampire, and you think you can smooth it over with ice cream?"

"So you don't want the ice cream?" Mr. Van Heusen said.

"No, we want the ice cream," Mr. Russo replied.

"Jerry!" Mrs. Russo scolded her husband. It was clear that ice cream *wasn't* enough of an apology for her.

"And I also think we need more of an apology," Mr. Russo continued.

"How does unlimited toppings sound?" suggested Mrs. Van Heusen.

"I accept your apology," Mr. Russo said at once. "I'll take mine in a cup."

"Daddy!" Alex exclaimed. "They were just about to drink our blood!"

"That's right," Mr. Russo said, filled with outrage again. "This is unacceptable. Harper was going to be the one to take care of us in our old age."

"Yes," Harper said to herself, making a mental note.

"All right. I'll make dinner, too," proposed Mr. Van Heusen. "Who is up for some really rare steaks?"

Everyone in the room cheered—until Mrs.

Russo spoke up. "Okay, but you have to start with a salad," she insisted. "No French fries. No butter. And water instead of soda."

Alex turned to the Van Heusens. "Would somebody *please* bite her?" she asked.

Chapter Seven

After dinner at the Late Nite Bite, the Russos and Juliet went back to the loft to hang out.

"You are totally checking out my neck," Justin teased Juliet.

"No, I'm not!" she protested. "I had a big breakfast."

"You are so cute!" Justin said.

"No, you are," replied Juliet.

"Nose kiss!" Justin sang out. He leaned close to Juliet so that they could touch their noses together.

"Ugh," Alex groaned from across the room. "We're trying to enjoy some pumpkin pie here."

By "some" pumpkin pie, Alex meant the biggest pumpkin pie the world had ever seen. Mrs. Russo had had to do *something* with the hundreds of pounds of pumpkin guts they had scooped out of Max's pumpkin house after destroying it. She wouldn't tell anyone exactly what ingredients she'd used to make the pie, but it was so delicious that Alex suspected the pie was full of sugar and butter.

Which was absolutely fine with her. If Mrs. Russo was forgetting about her health food kick, Alex certainly wasn't going to remind her!

"You know, we're going to have to eat this whole thing, because it won't fit in the fridge," Mr. Russo said. "Hand me that big spoon."

"Jerry, that's a shovel," Mrs. Russo pointed out.

"I know what it's called," replied Mr. Russo. He grabbed a gardening trowel off the table and began to eat a giant hunk of pie off it.

At that moment, Max walked into the room, followed by the satellite guy, who was carrying a giant satellite dish.

Max's mouth dropped open when he saw his family huddled around the massive pumpkin pie. "You're eating my house! Aw, man!" he groaned. Then he turned to the satellite guy and said, "Can you install that on a helmet so I can always watch TV?"

Alex added another dollop of whipped cream to her piece of pie. She wanted to feel sorry for Max about losing his pumpkin house.

But she couldn't. The delicious pie was way worth it!

PART
THREE

Chapter One

There were two things Alex Russo loved a lot. Well, there were more than two, but at the moment, two in particular stood out. She loved hanging out at Betty's and Fleming's, an insanely fun restaurant that combined great food and awesome arcade games. And she loved hanging out with Dean Moriarty, one of the cutest—and coolest—guys she'd ever met. Not to mention a great boyfriend.

Hanging out *with* Dean at Betty's and Fleming's? Now that was bliss!

As always, Betty's and Fleming's was packed with kids playing games and chowing down on burgers and fries. Alex and Dean had snagged a great table that was attached to a skee ball machine. Alex stood at the base of the skee ball machine, eyeing the ball in her hands, her face a mask of concentration. She wanted her aim to be perfect so that after she threw the ball, it would land right in the 100-point cup—the most difficult goal in skee ball.

Dean stood behind her and stretched his arm along hers. He cupped his hand around Alex's hand. "Keep your arm steady," Dean advised. "Aim. Follow through."

As he spoke, Dean guided Alex's movements as she threw the ball. It arced through the air—and landed in the 100-point cup!

"Oh, my goodness, one hundred points!"

Alex squealed, her brown eyes shining with delight.

"Nice going, Russo," Dean said with a grin. A very cute and charming grin. "Try it on your own this time."

"On my own? Oh, no," Alex replied. "Now I'm torn between admitting that I've gotten pretty good at skee ball and wanting you to keep doing that cuddly guiding-my-arm thing you were doing."

Dean smiled as he took Alex's hand and led her over to sit at their table. Apparently, he didn't like the idea of making his Alex feel torn. "Let's get something to eat," he suggested instead. In one smooth movement, Dean tilted the touch screen at the table toward himself and began to tap on it.

"Welcome to Betty's and Fleming's." A cool robotic voice sounded from the machine. "Please tap in your order."

"I'll order for you," Dean said to Alex. "It's

more romantic." He began to tap the touch screen as he verbally confirmed her order. "Barbecue bacon burger with curly fries in the bun, and a double chocolate shake, whipped cream on the bottom?"

"You know me," Alex said in a dreamy voice as she closed her eyes. "Doesn't it freak you out how perfect we are together?"

They were like those couples you saw in movies or read about in books. The ones whose love was so deep, so timeless . . .

"Nah, I don't think about it," Dean replied. Alex's dreamy look vanished. "Because then I'd be thinking instead of enjoying it."

"Dean, you made sense!" Alex gushed, once again looking pleased. "This is the best date ever. Do that thing I think is cool."

Dean smiled at her as he flip-snapped his fingers.

"I *love* that!" Alex sighed happily. Alex's "best date ever" was like a perfect dream come true.

Which was really pretty accurate.

Suddenly, an alarm began beeping.

Not just any alarm—an alarm clock.

Dean, who had actually been sound asleep in his bedroom and not hanging at Betty's and Fleming's, woke up with a start. "Cool dream," he mumbled as he rubbed his eyes. Then he grabbed his cell phone to check the time. "Oh, man, I'm late for school. Guess I'll try again tomorrow." Dean rolled over and went back to sleep. School could wait. He wanted to get back to Betty's and Fleming's.

Meanwhile, many miles away, in the living room of the Russo loft, Alex smiled. Her grin was hidden by the magical dream helmet she wearing. The helmet gave her the power to enter another person's dreams.

Love had been in the air ever since Alex's brother, Justin, had started dating Juliet Van Heusen, a pretty girl who just happened to be a vampire. While Alex wasn't that interested in dating a vampire—especially since she had narrowly escaped a vampire attack from Juliet's parents—she did miss going out and having fun with a cute guy like Dean. Since he had moved away, she'd been feeling a little lonely.

Not to mention it was *more* than a little weird (and annoying) for Justin to have more of a social life than she did!

So Alex solved the problem in the easiest way she could: with a little magic. Sometimes being a wizard really came in handy. As did having a dream helmet. By slipping it on her head, Alex could enter anyone's dreams—and control what happened in them!

"See you in your dreams tomorrow night, Dean," she said now as she took off the helmet.

Alex wasn't alone. Her best friend, Harper Evans, was sitting on the couch, flipping through a magazine.

"Harper! What are you doing here?" Alex asked, surprised. She'd been alone when she put the helmet on.

"Waiting for you to stop using the dream helmet," Harper replied. "Hurry up. We'll be late for school. They chained down the trash cans, so we can't walk in as one again."

"Harper, I just had another perfect date with Dean!" Alex said as the girls set off for their school, Tribeca Prep. "He ordered for me at the touch-screen place, and—"

"Dean moved away months ago," Harper interrupted Alex. "You've got to stop using magic to date him in his dreams. It's just wrong."

Sometimes being Alex's best friend was a tough job. Dealing with boys was difficult enough. Add magic, and it was nearly impossible. Still, she was her best friend, and best friends helped each other out, no matter what.

"Why?" Alex asked. "I go into his dreams and control everything so it's exactly the way I want. Since Dean moved away, our relationship has never been better!"

"Do you ever listen to yourself, or is there

some invisible shield that blocks your words from your ears?" Harper retorted.

"You're just mad because I went to Betty's and Fleming's without you," Alex pointed out to her friend.

"No, I'm not," Harper said. "Touch-screen ordering? It's dehumanizing when a robot gets your order wrong. And if we don't watch out, robots are going to unite and take over *every-thing*!"

Alex's eyes sparkled mischievously. "How do you know I'm not one—I'm not one—I'm not one—" she said mimicking a malfunctioning robot.

Harper's mouth dropped open. "It's happening already!" she shrieked, and ran off to school as fast as she could.

Alex laughed. It was worth walking the rest of the way to school alone to see Harper overreact about something as silly as a robot takeover!

Chapter Two

That evening, Justin and Juliet went to the movies. True, their relationship had gotten off to a rocky start when their parents had forbidden them to date. (It hadn't helped that their parents owned rival sandwich restaurants.) But ever since Juliet helped save Alex and Harper from being attacked by her vampire parents, things had smoothed out. Now they were better than ever.

Night had fallen as Justin walked Juliet home from the movie theater. But despite the hour, the streets of Greenwich Village, where both the Russos and the Van Heusens lived, were crowded with people eating at outdoor cafés, going to parties, and enjoying the New York City nightlife.

"*Tears of Blood* totally rocked!" Juliet exclaimed. "And I'm not saying that just because I'm a vampire and I love anything that has to do with blood."

"I had so much fun with you that I completely ignored my self-prescribed bedtime," Justin replied with a yawn. "I'm going to get thirty-seven minutes less sleep than usual. Totally worth it!"

Juliet smiled and then grew thoughtful. Finally, she spoke. "Justin, my family and I are going away on vacation," Juliet said. "And I don't want to be away from you for that long. So . . . I was wondering if you want to come with us to the lake?"

"Oh, uh, that would be great," Justin stammered, suddenly feeling a little light-headed. This was a big step. A really big step. "Sure. But if I go away with your family, will it be to Lake Sukkanek?"

Juliet laughed, despite herself. Then she tried to look stern. "We don't like corny vampire jokes," she reminded him firmly. "But that's a good one. Anyway, I was hoping you'd come, because it'll be really fun."

"Yeah, it will," Justin said. He tried to match Juliet's enthusiasm. "I'm going to ask my parents. I mean, they can't still treat me like I'm a kid. They can't say I'm not ready to go away with my girlfriend and her family. I sleep in pitch black now! In fact, I prefer it!"

When they reached the Late Nite Bite, Justin said good-bye to Juliet. Then he continued walking to his family's restaurant, the Waverly Sub Station, which was only a block away, his mind reeling. A vacation with the Van Heusens was not on his top-five to-do list. Not yet, anyway. He had to come up with an escape plan, fast. He just hoped his parents would help.

Later that night, Alex and Harper were hanging out in one of the booths of the restaurant, while Mr. Russo arranged the menus. Justin was in the middle of telling his dad about the Van Heusen family vacation.

"So, it would be for the whole weekend. But if you don't want me to go, I totally understand." He tried to sound nonchalant. Like he actually wanted his dad to say . . .

"Sure, you can go with Juliet and the Van Heusens," Mr. Russo replied right away.

Justin blinked a few times. What? No! That was not the right answer. "I won't even be mad," he assured his father.

"It sounds like fun!" Mr. Russo continued. "Juliet's a sweet girl."

"I get it," Justin said, nodding. "You don't want me to go."

Mr. Russo stopped stacking menus and looked up at his son. "Justin, I'm giving you my permission to go away with your vampire girlfriend. As long as you hang upside down in different rooms," Mr. Russo said, cracking up at his own joke.

But Justin didn't think it was very funny. "Great," he said. "But we should probably ask Mom, huh? She might think that Juliet and I are getting too serious too fast. But we're not. Even though a lot of people and parenting books would say that we are."

Mr. Russo stopped laughing. "Justin, you've got to stop buying me those parenting books," he said seriously. "I'm not going to read them."

Justin sighed as he headed upstairs to his

bedroom. His father was a lost cause.

Just then, the bell on the restaurant door jangled as someone stepped inside. Harper looked up to see who it was. Her mouth dropped open. "Dean's here?" she gasped. "Alex, are we in one of your dream dates right now?"

"Dean?" Alex asked as she spun around to see for herself.

"It must be your dream!" Harper whispered excitedly. "Oh, my gosh! Can I control what I do, or do you control everything? Can I drink this if I want to?" Harper reached across the table and grabbed Alex's soda. Then she took a big gulp. Wow! "It tastes like real root beer! Everything is so vibrant!"

Alex wasn't paying any attention to Harper—and she didn't even notice that Harper had stolen her soda. This was no dream. "Oh, my gosh! It's really Dean! He's really here!"

As Dean walked over to their booth, Alex

tried to act cool. Unfortunately, he had over-heard her.

"Yep, it's really me, Russo," Dean said with a grin. He turned to Harper and nodded.

"Moriarty," Harper replied coolly. "It's been long enough. I believe a friendly hug is in order."

But as Dean held open his arms, Harper changed her mind. "I'm not ready," she said as she sat back down.

"What are you doing here?" Alex asked when she got over the initial shock of seeing her long-distance boyfriend up close and personal.

"I've been thinking about you a lot lately," Dean replied. "And you've been in a lot of my dreams. So I took my vacation days from school a little early."

Harper rolled her eyes. "You don't get vacation days from school," she pointed out. "*This* is why I don't hug you."

But Alex didn't care that Dean had an . . . unconventional understanding of how school worked.

In fact, that was one of her favorite things about him! *And* he'd come to see her! Another one of her favorite things about him!

Chapter Three

The next day, Justin hung out near the Late Nite Bite, keeping an eye out for Juliet. Max had followed Justin and was trying to keep an eye on the corner hot-dog vendor—without being noticed.

"Hey, Justin!" Juliet said when she saw him "Did you talk to your dad? Can you go?"

Justin tried to look upset. "Uh, yeah, I talked to him. He said . . . no. I can't go," he replied.

"Really?" Juliet asked, her voice filled with disappointment.

"I can't believe it, either!" Justin said, shaking his head. "He reads all these parenting books, and apparently it's not a good idea. And I got so mad, and he got this serious look on his face and said, 'No way, Justin—and don't bring it up again.' So if you see him, don't bring it up." He stopped and took a deep breath.

"Did he say why?" Juliet asked.

"Oh, I don't know," Justin lied. "Some talk about us getting too serious too fast."

"Well, we *are* getting kind of serious," Juliet agreed.

"And I am *fine* with it!" Justin exclaimed. "But you know parents. They get all serious about getting serious."

Juliet smiled sadly at Justin. "Well, I'm going to miss you," she said with a sigh. "I'd better get to work."

"Okay, I'll see you later," Justin replied.

As Juliet walked back into the Late Nite Bite, Justin let out a sigh of relief. He didn't like lying to her. But it felt like the only option. The other choice was just too . . . serious.

"Why aren't you going away with your girlfriend?" Max asked his brother.

"I don't know . . ." Justin said slowly. "Relationships are way more complicated than you can understand."

"You don't think I have relationship problems?" Max asked, folding his arms across his chest. "I've got a world of trouble with that hot-dog lady! Now, if you'll excuse me . . ."

Max walked up to the hot-dog vendor. "The usual, please," he said politely.

The hot-dog lady placed a hot dog in a bun and squirted mustard all over it.

"Mustard? Again?" Max asked angrily. "What is going on? You *know* the usual has ketchup!"

"Right. Sorry," replied the hot-dog vendor in a bored voice. She handed Max a new hot dog that was covered with ketchup. Max took the hot dog, but he didn't move out of the line.

"We've got to figure out what's happening between us," he said earnestly.

"I figured out what's happening," the hot-dog lady replied matter-of-factly. Max perked up. "You're holding up the line. Next!"

Max sadly shook his head as he stepped away. "How did we get here?"

It was clear that both Russo boys were having romantic troubles. Hopefully, Alex would have better luck with her love life now that she could date Dean in real life—and not just in his dreams.

Later that day, Alex and Dean went on a date to Betty's and Fleming's. A *real* date, not a dream one. Alex grinned as they snagged the same table and skee ball machine they'd used during Dean's dream. Not many people got a chance to have a dream come true—and Alex planned to enjoy every minute of it! She didn't even care that she'd had to spend more time than usual styling her long brown hair so that it would look just as good as it did when she appeared in Dean's dreams. Or that she had to make sure her outfit was different—but just as cute—as the one she'd worn the other night. Alex didn't mind the extra effort, as long as the real-life date was as fantastic as the dream date.

It got off to a good—and familiar—start. Dean stepped right up to the skee ball machine and began to play. He threw ball after ball, making plenty of great shots. The machine spat out a long row of prize tickets with every point Dean earned.

"Yes! I nailed it!" Dean cheered for himself.

"Okay, you've won enough tickets to get a pencil sharpener," Alex said at last. "Let me have a turn."

But instead of gallantly stepping aside to give Alex a turn, Dean just smirked. "Come on, Russo," he said as he grabbed another ball. "You know you're not good at skee ball."

Alex frowned. That wasn't what he was supposed to say. Still, she wasn't going to give up yet. "But maybe you could show me by guiding my arm, kind of cuddly, like this," Alex suggested as she demonstrated for Dean.

But Dean ignored her and threw the ball on his own. "Sweet!" he cheered. "I beat my own record. Let's eat!"

Alex sighed as she and Dean sat down at their table. Just like before, Dean tilted the touch screen toward himself. And just like before, he began to tap on it.

"Welcome to Betty's and Fleming's," the robotic voice said. "Please tap in your order."

"Oh, are you ordering for me?" Alex asked hopefully. This was perfect. . . .

"No, I'm playing Bonko," Dean replied, not even bothering to glance up from the screen. "Shoot! I bonked out. I'm going again. You got any money left on your game card?"

"Dean!" Alex said, putting her hand on his arm. "You're not really paying attention to me."

"What do you mean?" Dean asked. "I'm here, aren't I?"

"Yeah, but we haven't seen each other in months, and you're more interested in that stupid Bonko," Alex pointed out.

"Okay, fine," Dean sighed. He tilted the touch screen toward Alex. "Why don't you order your food?"

"You want me to order for myself?" Alex replied. "Why don't you order for me?"

"No, you order for me," Dean said. "I'm going to get my pencil sharpener from the prize tent."

"This is a *date*, Dean," Alex said firmly.

"We're staying together." She started to tap her order into the touch screen. "Barbecue bacon burger, curly fries inside the bun, and a double chocolate shake with whipped cream on the bottom."

Frowning, Dean pulled the screen away from her and began tapping on it. "You've got to stop eating like that," he lectured Alex. "A big hunk of meat will just wreck your heart."

"Yeah," Alex said, shaking her head sadly. "That's not all that's wrecking my heart."

"I've been telling you to eat healthier," Dean said as he continued to tap the screen, unaware of her growing anger. "I just ordered a Cobb salad. Let me know when it gets here. Bonko!"

Alex slumped into a corner of the booth as Dean began to play yet another round of Bonko. This date wasn't turning out like the dream at all.

It was more like a nightmare!

Chapter Four

The next day, Alex found Harper in the hall at Tribeca Prep. "Well, it turns out you were right," Alex said.

"I knew it!" Harper exclaimed. "I'm in your dream! Can I fly?"

Alex shook her head. "Harper, this isn't a dream," she said. "You were right about me and Dean. We've grown apart, and I've been fooling myself by going into his dreams."

"And you only made it worse, because you created Dream Dean and now you expect Real Dean to be someone that he's not," Harper said wisely.

"I *said* you were right," Alex said, annoyed at how much sense Harper was making. She didn't need to rub it in. "See, a lot of times you're right—and this is exactly why I don't tell you."

"So what are you going to do?" Harper asked.

"I've got to do what I should have done when he moved," Alex said with a sigh. "Break up with him."

"Oooh," Harper said, looking at Alex with pity. "Breaking up is always hard."

"How do you know?" Alex asked.

Though Alex had a point, Harper frowned. She never appreciated it when Alex pointed out the nonexistent status of her love life. "You're making it hard to be supportive," she told her friend.

"You're right, though," Alex continued, unconcerned. "Breaking up with Dean will be hard. I mean, I don't want to hurt his feelings. Ugh. This would be so much easier if he broke up with me."

"Hey, that's a good idea!" Harper exclaimed. "Get him to break up with you!"

"Yeah, I could do that," Alex said slowly as she thought it over.

"But it will be a challenge to make him want to break up with you," Harper pointed out. "You're awesome."

Alex grinned. "I like you," she said.

"Oh, that's such a relief!" Harper exclaimed.

"Really?" Alex asked.

"I get a little insecure once in a while," Harper replied. "But I'm back!"

While Alex and Harper were busy plotting the breakup, Juliet was plotting a makeup. Things with Justin had seemed a little weird since she had invited him on vacation, and she wanted to fix it. She didn't want him to feel bad that he couldn't go. That was his dad's fault.

After school that day, she went to the Waverly Sub Station to see Justin. Mr. Russo was waiting on a few tables of people who'd stopped in for an afternoon snack.

"Hi, Mr. Russo," she said as she walked up to the counter. "Is Justin around?"

"I haven't seen him," Mr. Russo replied, shaking his head. "He must be packing for his big trip."

"Why would he be packing?" Juliet asked, confused. "He can't go."

"He can't go?" repeated Mr. Russo. "He'll be sorry to hear that. He was really excited."

"I know," Juliet said. "So why can't he go?"

"I don't know," Mr. Russo said with a shrug. "You didn't tell me."

Mr. Russo and Juliet stared at each other for

a long moment. Neither one understood what the other was saying.

Finally, Juliet said, "*You're* the one who said he can't go. *I* don't care what those parenting books say."

"Me neither!" Mr. Russo agreed at once.

"So you didn't say no?" Juliet asked.

"No," Mr. Russo said. "I mean, yes, I didn't say no. Are we clear here?"

Juliet nodded sadly. It all made perfect sense now. "You said yes and he said no."

Just then, Justin got home from school. He dropped his heavy backpack on the floor. "Oh, hey," he said when he saw Juliet. He started to grin.

But Juliet's cold glare froze the smile right off his face.

"Why did you say you couldn't go on vacation when you could?" she demanded.

"And why did you tell people I read those parenting books?" Mr. Russo asked with his hands on his hips. He sounded just as upset as Juliet.

"Um . . . because . . . I didn't think this moment would happen," Justin mumbled as he tried—and failed—to think of a good excuse for lying to his girlfriend. "Because if I did, I probably wouldn't have done it."

"If you didn't want to go with me, you should've just said so," Juliet said, sounding hurt.

"I'm sorry, Juliet," Justin replied. "I wasn't thinking. It's probably because of the thirty-seven minutes of sleep I lost. I'm not good with less than eight hours of sleep. It's terrible!"

"I guess you're not good with more than eight hours of sleep, either," Juliet said. "It's terrible."

And without another word, Juliet walked out of the restaurant, leaving a heartbroken Justin behind. He turned to his dad for a word of support or encouragement—anything to make him feel better about ruining the best relationship he'd ever had.

But Mr. Russo was too annoyed with Justin's lies. "Parenting books!" he muttered, shaking his head in disgust.

There was no doubt that Justin had made a giant mess of things. And now he'd have to find a way to fix it.

He just hoped he could!

Chapter Five

Juliet stormed out of the Waverly Sub Station, filled with hurt and anger about catching Justin in a lie. He didn't really want to go on vacation with her, after all. How could that be? They seemed so happy together.

She hadn't gone far before she ran into another member of the Russo family. Max was sitting right outside the restaurant, eating a hot dog and trying to catch the attention of the hot-dog vendor on the corner.

"Hey, Juliet," Max mumbled around a mouthful of hot dog.

"Hey, Max," Juliet replied. "What are you doing?"

"I'm eating a hot dog, but it's not from *that* vendor," Max announced loudly. "It's from *another* vendor."

He hoped his disloyalty to the local hot-dog vendor would make her jealous—or would at least make her notice him and therefore get his order right. But, as usual, the hot-dog lady ignored him.

"She's jealous! I know it!" Max yelled. But he couldn't even fool himself this time. Max sighed and looked at his feet. "It's over."

"Hey, do you want me to bite her neck for you?" Juliet offered.

"Nah," Max replied. Then his face brightened. "But now that I know that's an option, there are some people I'd like to talk about."

"Make a list!" Juliet suggested. Then she had an idea. "Maybe *you* can help *me* with something. How do you get your brother to tell you what's really on his mind?"

"Oh, I use randomness," Max replied.

"What?" Juliet asked. She didn't understand what Max meant by "randomness"—but she was ready to learn more.

"Yeah, I just say random things, and while people are trying to figure it out, they say stuff that's on their mind," Max said. "Have you ever noticed pineapples never wear bathrobes?"

Juliet looked confused. "Why would you say that?" she asked. "I mean, we were just talking about how Justin doesn't want to go on vacation, and I'm upset about it, because I think I'm in love with him!"

Suddenly, Juliet knew *exactly* what Max meant by "randomness." "Hey!" she said, her voice full of admiration. "That random thing really works."

"What? What random thing?" Max asked. "I haven't even done it yet."

Juliet smiled at Justin's little brother. He was a weird kid, but he'd just given her all the tools she needed to get inside Justin's head and hopefully save their relationship! She couldn't wait to try it out—as soon as she returned from her family vacation.

Chapter Six

Back at the Russos' loft, Alex and Harper were hanging out in the living room. They had spent the entire afternoon trying to come up with a plan to convince Dean to break up with Alex so that she wouldn't have to break up with him first.

"Okay, how about this idea?" Harper finally suggested. "Dean will totally break up with you if you wear something totally repulsive."

Alex took a long look at Harper's outfit. "But then what are you going to wear?" she asked.

Harper was used to people not appreciating her creative fashion sense, so Alex's insult didn't bother her at all. "I wasn't talking about *this* outfit," she said patiently.

"No, I know." Alex quickly tried to cover up her insensitive remark. "I meant, I'm going to use a spell to make me a slob! No one wants to go out with someone gross!"

Alex grabbed her wand and quickly cast a spell. "*What I need now is the opposite of clean, make me a girl without hygiene!*" she chanted.

Poof!

A blinding flash of light filled the room as Alex was transformed. Her hair was suddenly greasy, matted into thick clumps. Her eyebrows were overgrown and bushy. Her frumpy clothes were covered in food stains. Even her breath stank!

"Whoa!" exclaimed Harper, waving a hand in front of her nose. "You are hideous!"

"Awesome!" Alex cheered as she checked out her new look in the mirror. "It worked!"

"Okay, normally I'd stay and check out whatever flies out of that nest on your head, but you reek," Harper said as she walked backward toward the door. "Keep your arms down, please."

Harper swung open the door, just as Dean was about to knock on it.

"Hey, Harper, what's up?" asked Dean.

"Your chances of getting a rash!" Harper said as she hurried away.

"Hi, baby," Alex cooed as Dean walked into the room.

Dean took one glance at Alex, and a look of horror crossed his face. "Oh, man," he said. "I'm going to try to say this as nicely as I can: you look like something I snaked out of my shower drain."

Alex grinned, revealing a mouthful of yellow, crooked teeth. Her plan was working! "I held myself together for our date, but this is really the way I am," she said with a shrug. Dean couldn't see how pleased she was by his grossed-out reaction. That would blow her cover. "Pretty disgusting, huh?"

"Yeah," Dean agreed. "You are."

"Makes you not want to be near me," Alex said. "I get it."

"No, *I* get it," Dean said. "This is because of me."

"Well, yes," Alex said. She didn't quite follow what Dean meant. Did he know she had made herself ugly on purpose?

"Since I left, you've been overwhelmed with sadness—and you just let yourself go," Dean continued. "I've seen people like you on talk shows. But I'm going to help you get back on track. Where's the floss?"

"What? No!" Alex replied, panic creeping

into her voice as her plan started to backfire in a big way. "Look, Dean. That's not what I want."

"Of course not," Dean said soothingly. "And you probably don't want a warm washcloth behind the ears. Now, where's your washcloth? Do you even *own* a washcloth?"

"I thought you'd see me like this and want to break up!" Alex groaned. She could only think of one thing worse than continuing to date Dean: getting a makeover from him!

"You want to break up?" Dean asked.

"Well, now that you bring it up, since it's your idea and all . . . maybe we should," Alex replied, crossing her fingers that Dean would take the hint.

"Okay," Dean said with a shrug. "Then let's break up."

Alex watched in shock as Dean started to leave. Wait a minute! He didn't seem upset that their relationship was over—at all! "Uh, really?" she asked. "That was easy. That was *really* easy. That was really, *really* easy!"

"No big deal," Dean said. "See you."

As Dean walked out, Alex flopped down on the couch, utterly dejected. "What *was* that?" she said to the empty room.

Alex had gotten exactly what she wanted. Her relationship with Dean was over. She hadn't had to do the dumping, and he seemed totally fine about it—not crushed or heartbroken at all.

So, why did she feel so upset?

Chapter Seven

While Alex tried to reverse the spell she'd cast—her bad breath and body odor were starting to bother her as much as Dean's behavior—Justin sat in a booth in the restaurant downstairs. He wasn't in much better shape . . . although he did smell better.

Justin needed advice. He needed to talk.

He needed his dad.

When Justin saw Mr. Russo coming toward

his booth, he started to smile. He was sure that his dad would be able to help him figure out how to fix the mess he'd made with Juliet. "Hey, Dad," Justin said in a sad voice. "I guess you noticed how down I am and you wanted to talk."

But Mr. Russo hadn't noticed anything like that. "No, we need the table," he said, distracted.

Then Justin's words sunk in. "Okay, we'll talk," Mr. Russo replied as he slid into the booth.

Justin took a deep breath. "Dad, I lied to Juliet and now she's mad," he explained.

"Yeah, about that," Mr. Russo began. "Why didn't you want to go on vacation? You really like Juliet."

"I know, but I've never been in a relationship this long and going on vacation with her family seems serious and it's happening kind of fast," Justin said in a rush.

"Aha!" exclaimed Mr. Russo as he started to understand. "So you're afraid."

"Yeah—and you were no help," Justin said. "You were ready to pack a bag for me!"

"Justin, I know going away with a girl's family is a big step," Mr. Russo said. "I said yes because I think you're ready. Having your first serious girlfriend is part of growing up."

"Man," Justin muttered as he buried his head in his hands. His dad was right. "I really messed up."

Mr. Russo smiled kindly. "Messing up? That's also a part of growing up. I'm *still* growing up. Ask your mother."

"So what do I do now?" Justin asked.

"Tell her you want to go on the vacation," Mr. Russo advised his son.

"But they already left," Justin said, sounding more depressed than ever.

"Here," Mr. Russo said as he tossed a set of keys to Justin.

But Justin didn't see the keys coming. They bounced off the side of his head!

"Ow!" Justin exclaimed. "Hey, I feel bad enough. Stop throwing things at me!"

"Those are the keys to the flying carpet," Mr. Russo explained. "See if you can catch up with her."

Justin grinned at his father. Yes! He would do this! It was just the kind of romantic gesture he needed to try and win Juliet back.

"Thanks, Dad!" he said gratefully as he hurried out of the restaurant.

Mr. Russo stood up and waved to some customers standing in the doorway. "Okay, party of two," he called. "Your table is ready. Sit down quickly before any of my other kids come in with a problem!"

Just then, Max sauntered through the room wearing a giant hot-dog costume, complete with wavy red lines of "ketchup" down the middle. The customers took one look at him and hurried into the booth, taking Mr. Russo's suggestion seriously

But Max didn't even notice. He had a plan to patch things up with the hot-dog vendor, and he couldn't wait to put it into action!

He went outside and walked right up to the hot-dog lady, who was standing on her usual corner. "I know we've had out problems, but I really want to work it out," Max said earnestly.

"Okay," replied the hot-dog lady, not looking up from the relish jar. "Do you want to pass out fliers?"

"If that's what it takes," Max vowed.

"All right," the hot-dog lady agreed. "One usual coming up. And nice gesture, wearing that hot-dog suit for me."

"Oh, this?" asked Max, looking down at his costume. "It's not for you. It's for something I'm doing later."

The hot-dog lady shook her head and

decided not to ask for more information. The kid was going to pass out advertising fliers for free—why mess with that?

Alex, having reversed the spell so that her hideous transformation had worn off, finally ventured outside. She sat on a bench nearby with Harper in the warm afternoon. But Alex couldn't enjoy the gorgeous day; she felt too overwhelmed by her mixed-up feelings about the breakup with Dean.

She spilled every detail to Harper. "And then I said I wanted to break up, he agreed, and walked out," Alex finished. "I mean, what was that?"

Harper was confused, too—but not about Dean's reaction to the breakup. "I don't get it," she said. "You *wanted* to break up, and you did. Mission accomplished, right?"

"Yeah, sure, I got what I wanted," Alex tried to explain. "But I guess I thought he'd fight for me. I mean, we had a history together, and he just—let it go."

"Well, it was a pretty convincing spell," Harper pointed out. "And you know that Dean doesn't talk a lot, say what he's thinking, or share much." She paused. "Exactly *what* do you see in him?"

"I don't know," Alex said miserably. "But Dream Dean was great at expressing himself."

"But he wasn't real," Harper said patiently. "And you were controlling it."

"I know," Alex admitted. "And it was wrong."

There was silence as both girls thought about the situation.

Finally, Harper spoke up. "You know I'm against this, but you could go back into Dean's dream one more time and get the breakup you really want."

Alex's face brightened immediately. "You're awesome!" she exclaimed.

Harper shrugged. "I like you," she replied.

"Oh, that's a relief," Alex said sincerely.

Harper was completely shocked. Could it be that Alex—confident, self-assured Alex—felt insecure sometimes, like a normal person? "Really?" asked Harper.

Alex grinned and nodded. Now she had a dream to get to.

Chapter Eight

That night, when the loft was quiet and all the other Russos were fast asleep, Alex slipped on the dream helmet one more time. She instantly found herself hanging out with Dean at Betty's and Fleming's again.

"Hey, Russo," Dean said when Alex appeared.

"Hey, Dean," replied Alex. "Listen, most of the time I come into your dreams and control everything. But this time it's *your* dream. You can say and do whatever you want."

"I can?" Dean asked with a grin. "Cool."

Poof!

There was a bright flash of light as President Abraham Lincoln materialized in the middle of Betty's and Fleming's!

Alex turned to Dean. "Abraham Lincoln?" she asked, surprised.

"Yeah," Dean said with a shrug. "It's my dream, and in my dreams, I like to have the sixteenth president as my wingman. So what's up, Russo?"

Alex decided to get right to the point—even if President Lincoln was listening in. "I wanted to talk about our breakup," she said.

"I don't know," Dean said at once.

President Lincoln cleared his throat. "Go ahead, Dean," he said in a deep voice. "Tell her how you really feel. It's best for you to be honest."

Dean frowned. "You know that's hard for me, Mr. One-Six," he said quietly.

"I'll let you wear my stovepipe hat," offered President Lincoln.

Dean knew that he had to be honest with Alex on his own—without any help from the sixteenth president of the United States. He faced Alex and took a deep breath. "Okay. Here it is. I couldn't be real when we broke up, because it was too painful," he said at last.

Alex's eyes grew wide. "It was?" she asked.

"Yeah, it was," replied Dean. "I've never known anyone like you. The only way I could get through it was to tell you it was 'no big deal.' You'll always be my first love, Alex. That's one thing that will never change."

"Same here," Alex said. She smiled sadly at Dean. Breaking up with him wasn't easy— even in a dream—but this way was a little more satisfying than how the breakup had played out in real life.

In his dream, Dean handed Alex a red rose.

"Good-bye, Dean," Alex said.

"Good-bye, Alex," he replied.

But before Dean could leave, there was something that Alex wanted to do first. She reached over to President Lincoln and grabbed the stovepipe hat off his head. Then she turned to Dean and put the hat squarely on his head. She figured that any guy who'd dream about having Abe Lincoln as his wingman would want the chance to wear his hat.

And, after all, he'd earned it.

As Dean and the stovepipe hat faded away, Alex turned back to President Lincoln. "Let's play some skee ball," she suggested.

After all, there was no point in wasting a perfectly good dream at Betty's and Fleming's!

Meanwhile, Justin flew the magic carpet through the dark night as fast as he could toward Juliet's vacation destination. He had

had to wait until sundown to leave so that no ordinary humans would spot a flying carpet in the sky. That had only made him all the more anxious to reach Juliet as soon as possible.

And then, he found her. Far out in the country, beyond the bright city lights, he saw a dark figure flying in the sky, silhouetted against a full moon. Too big to be a bird and way too small to be aircraft, Justin knew at once that it had to be Juliet—flying with a pair of velvety black bat wings.

Justin grinned. Bat wings? He'd thought he couldn't love Juliet any more than he already did.

Clearly, he'd been wrong.

"Juliet, wait up!" he yelled as he flew the magic carpet even faster.

At the sound of her name, Juliet turned around. "Justin!" she said when she saw him flying up to her.

"My dad loaned me the flying carpet," Justin explained.

"I'm so glad you came!" she exclaimed. "I have to tell you something. Remember when you said you loved me?"

Justin was glad it was dark so that Juliet couldn't see him start to blush. It was also nice because it meant he couldn't quite see how batlike she looked. Bats were cool, but having a heart-to-heart with one was a little much. Even for a wizard like himself.

"Yeah, *that* was embarrassing," he mumbled.

"No, it's not, because I love you, too," Juliet said eagerly.

Justin started to grin again. "What? I can't hear you. Come closer."

Juliet smiled back at him as she flew over to the magic carpet. "I said, 'I love you, too,'" she repeated—even though she was pretty sure that Justin had heard her the first time.

"I love you, too, too," Justin replied. "Hey! We're getting pretty serious, and I'm not scared!"

Together, Justin and Juliet flew past the stars, past the moon, on their way to an amazing adventure. Justin wasn't worried at all about being in a serious relationship. Dating Juliet was like a dream come true—and he never wanted to wake up!

Back in Dean's dream, Alex was also enjoying an out-of-this-world dreamlike experience. After all, it wasn't every day that she got to challenge one of the greatest American presidents of all time to a fierce skee ball competition. And it wasn't every day that she got to *win* a skee ball competition—especially since her skee ball skills were pretty weak. But in dreams, anything was possible—especially when Alex was wearing the magical dream helmet!

"In your face, One-Six!" Alex cheered as she scored another hundred points. "In your face!"

PART
FOUR

Chapter One

It was the season. Prom season, to be precise. Prom meant dresses and tuxes, limos and dances. It meant magical evenings and romance. Usually.

At Tribeca Prep in New York City, the excitement about prom was out of control. Everyone was talking about it. Who would they ask? Who would be the DJ? Justin Russo was one of the students who couldn't wait for the big night. After all, he had a girlfriend now! He would be one of the big men on campus. And so what if his girlfriend happened to be a vampire. He was a wizard—who was he to judge?

Justin was so excited, in fact, that he was having trouble concentrating that afternoon after school. He was supposed to be helping out in the family restaurant, the Waverly Sub Station. But all he could think about was his girlfriend, Juliet Van Heusen. And the prom.

When Juliet walked into the restaurant, Justin nearly tackled her in his excitement. "Juliet, I'm glad you're here!" he exclaimed. "I wanted to ask you something. Will you go to my prom with me?"

Juliet smiled at her boyfriend, but shook her head. "Justin, that's sweet," she began. "But I'm a vampire, so I've been alive for a *long* time and I've been to *way* too many proms."

"How many?" Justin asked with a frown.

He didn't like the sound of this one bit.

"Five hundred and twenty-three," Juliet replied. She hated when Justin asked her age, but this was obviously important to him.

"Okay," he admitted, nodding. "That's a sizable number."

"Every prom, people expect too much, and then they're always let down," Juliet went on, her eyes going sort of hazy as she thought back on the many, many proms she had attended. The many, many lame dances she had endured. And, of course, the many, many horrible dresses she had donned.

"Not this time," Justin assured Juliet, breaking into her thoughts. "The theme of our prom is Best Night Ever!"

"There you go!" she said. "This one prom I went to . . . the theme was Starry Night. And there I was with this guy, Galileo . . ."

"The astronomer?" interrupted Justin, impressed.

"Is there another one?" Juliet asked him.

"I think there might be a rapper," Justin said as he thought about it. "Oh, no—that's Li'l Galileo."

Justin reached for Juliet's hand. He was not going to take no for an answer. "Juliet, if you go with me to prom, I will find a way to make it special," he vowed. "I *prom*-ise."

Juliet laughed. "Okay, I'll go," she said, finally giving in. "You won me over with your goofy play on words."

"People underestimate the power of goofy," Justin said confidently.

Suddenly, the door to the restaurant banged open as Justin's sister, Alex, rushed inside. She spotted her best friend, Harper Evans, across the restaurant and ran over to her. It wasn't hard to notice Harper. She had a unique fashion sense. Today she was wearing a weird black-and-white penguin-themed outfit that really made her stand out. And not in a good way.

But Alex was too excited to make fun of Harper's twisted fashion sense. "Harper, it's prom season!" she squealed, shoving a flier at her friend. "And look at the theme—Best Night Ever. Awesome!"

Harper began jumping up and down and clapping her hands together. "Oh, my gosh, I'm excited, too!" she exclaimed. "Sometimes I stifle my excitement in front of you, because you're rarely ever excited like this!" Then Harper paused. Something wasn't sitting right. Alex Russo didn't do proms. "Wait. Why are *you* excited about prom?"

"I'm not," Alex replied matter-of-factly. "I'm excited about you and me planning the *anti*-prom."

"I knew it," Harper said with a sigh as she sat down in the booth again. "I was excited about the wrong thing."

Alex ignored Harper's disappointment as she took a seat across from her. She had a plan. A great plan. "Look, for anti-prom we should go with a zombie theme," she announced. "Zombies move slow, but they're really scary. Slow but scary is the best combination in a monster . . . and a prom!" She sat back with a satisfied smile. Sometimes she was so brilliant, it scared her. And she wouldn't even have to use magic! Alex's parents really didn't like when she did that.

Harper let Alex's announcement sink in. Glancing across the room, she saw Justin's best friend, Zeke, hanging out. Her heart did a funny little jump. "Do you think Zeke would go with me?" Harper whispered to Alex.

Alex's eyes grew wide. "You like Zeke?" she asked in surprise. This was newsworthy information. Harper had been crushing on Justin for as long as she'd known him. But now that Justin was in a serious relationship with

Juliet, maybe Harper was ready to move on.

"Yeah, and I think he likes me, too!" Harper whispered excitedly. "I slipped and fell in the cafeteria, and he stepped around me like a gentleman."

"Hey, I pulled the enchiladas out of your hair. Don't *I* get any credit?" Alex replied, pretending to be hurt. Then she grinned at Harper. "Why don't you go ask him?"

Before Harper could protest, Alex grabbed her hand and pulled her out of the booth. Together, the two friends walked across the restaurant to Zeke.

"Zeke, we're planning a zombie prom on the same night as the regular prom," Harper blurted out. Oops! Not quite the smooth opening she had been going for.

"I love zombies," Zeke replied. "It's weird, but their slowness actually makes them scarier."

Alex nodded. He *so* got the theme. "What

do you think of turtles?" she asked.

Zeke shuddered. "Horrifying," he said.

Alex nodded again. Good answer.

Meanwhile, poor Harper was nervously biting her lip as she tried to muster all her courage to ask Zeke to the zombie prom. "I was wondering if you would like to . . . be on the committee to plan zombie prom?" she finally asked. "And maybe after we plan it, we could . . . be on the cleanup committee. And in between the planning and the cleaning, we might as well . . . stop by and make sure everyone's having a good time," she stammered.

"Are you asking me to be on three committees?" Zeke asked cheerfully. He grinned. Sounded fun to him. "Change my name to Extracurricular Man!"

Unaware that Harper had more to say, he left, crossing the restaurant to say hi to Justin. Harper turned to Alex and made a face. "I totally chickened out," she said miserably.

"The good news is you're dressed like a chicken," Alex pointed out, trying to look on the bright side.

Harper frowned. "This is a penguin," she corrected Alex.

"Oh. Then you penguined out!" Alex said, cracking up at her own joke.

Harper smiled at Alex. She might have lost her nerve and not asked Zeke to the zombie prom—but being on so many committees with him would definitely give her the chance to try again!

Chapter Two

Later that day, the two Russo boys were hanging out with their dad in the Wizard's Lair, beneath the Waverly Sub Station. The top secret room was where Mr. Russo gave his kids magic lessons to help them improve their wizard skills. It was full of amazing magical artifacts, too—from the dusty old magic carpet that could really fly, to the Wizard Emergency Kit, which was filled with important items like crystal-ball spackle, dragon extinguishers, and Wand-Aid for broken wands.

Mr. Russo had just finished rummaging around in the Wizard Emergency Kit, something he had to do pretty frequently when Max tried his hand at magic. He found some Wand-Aid and what looked like a regular screwdriver and began to repair Max's wand, which was broken in half. Tiny bright sparks fizzed around each broken end of the wand.

"This is why wands are not supposed to be kept in back pockets," Mr. Russo lectured as he applied more Wand-Aid. Justin and Max watched, impressed.

At last, Mr. Russo held up the wand, which was back in one piece. He proudly handed the repaired wand to Max.

"Thanks!" Max replied. "This baby's going in my front pocket!" At least, from now on. Max stood up so that he could slip the wand into the front pocket of his jeans. Then he sat back down.

Crack!

Max's wand snapped in half—again!

As Mr. Russo sighed and shook his head, a stack of wizard mail shot through the portal. Being a wizard had some fun perks—like magic portals that could transport stuff in the blink of an eye. Smiling, Justin walked over to get today's mail.

"Wizard mail's here," he announced as he began to sort the mail. "Here's a package for Max. And it's not from himself. He finally learned where to put the return address!"

Max grabbed the package from Justin and ripped it open. He read the letter inside. "Hey, I've been chosen to help trial-test a new wizard gadget, called a No Fear ring," Max announced. "They want me to see if it makes me fearless, then give them feedback. And they're going to pay me for it!"

Max shook the package until a strange-looking ring fell out. He picked it up and examined it closely. Very cool.

Mr. Russo picked up the rest of the paperwork that had been in the package. "I'll sign that permission slip and have the check sent to me," he said. "You know, to start paying me back for that new wand I'm going to buy."

Max nodded, but he wasn't paying much attention as he fiddled with the new ring. As he tried it on, he accidentally elbowed a glass beaker on the table—which fell to the floor and shattered.

Mr. Russo sighed. "I'll go get the Max Cleanup Cart." Having children was a full-time job!

Alex passed her dad as she walked into the lair, carrying a stack of fliers and a snack. "Hey, guys!" she announced. "I need to get the word out about zombie prom."

"Zombie prom?" Justin repeated. "Who would want to go to that? Juliet and I will be at Best Night Ever with all the *normal* people."

"Yes," Alex said sarcastically. "The wizard/vampire couple should *definitely* go to the normal-people prom. Have fun."

"Oh, we will," Justin replied. "What are you going to call your zombie prom? A Night to Dismember?"

Instead of being annoyed, Alex's face lit up. "Justin, that's great!" she exclaimed as she wrote it down. "Thanks!"

"Ugh!" groaned Justin. "I didn't mean to help you. Don't use it."

Ignoring her older brother, Alex turned to Max. "So, Max, you want to hand out these fliers around school?" she asked as she handed him the stack.

"I don't know . . ." Max said slowly. "I'm getting paid for this No Fear ring thing. So you should probably pay me for this."

"You mean, you'll have money, so you should pay me for letting you do it," Alex corrected him.

"Is that what I meant?" Max asked, confused.

"That's what you said," replied Alex.

"Okay, but can I pay you after I hand them out?" Max said.

"I should charge you extra for that," Alex sighed, pretending to be put out. It was so easy to mess with her little brother. "But I won't."

"Thanks!" Max said gratefully as Alex left the lair.

Excited about his new job, Max grabbed the No Fear ring-testing permission slip that Mr. Russo had signed and walked over to the portal. In one fast movement, Max dumped everything into the portal—the permission slip *and* the zombie prom fliers he had still been holding.

Whooosh!

The papers flew through the portal instantly, whisking their way off for delivery in the magic world.

"That permission slip seemed really heavy," Max said to himself. "Hey—where are those zombie fliers?"

Near midnight, when the Russo family was sound asleep in their loft, activity in the wizard world's cemetery was just starting to pick up. One by one, the coffins slowly creaked open as zombies emerged to hang out and play cards—slowly, of course. Very, very slowly.

A mummy mailman, trailing ancient bandages, lumbered through the graveyard, lugging a heavy bag of magical mail. He handed a flier for Alex's zombie prom to each and every zombie in the cemetery.

"Mail's here," drawled a zombie girl slowly. She looked down at the flier in her hand, and her eyes narrowed—sort of. As much as zombie eyes can narrow. "'Zombie prom?'" she read. "I'm not going. Last prom, I lost an arm."

"I love to dance," argued a zombie boy. "Come on, we never do anything fun anymore."

"Fine, I'll go," agreed the zombie girl. "But I'm *not* dancing."

And that was how word about the zombie prom spread through the zombie world. Alex Russo was in for a big surprise—bigger than she ever could have imagined!

Chapter Three

The next day after school, Alex and Max were helping Mr. Russo do some prep work in the kitchen to get ready for the dinner rush at the Waverly Sub Station. Alex sliced tomatoes thinly while Max washed bowls full of lettuce.

"Hey, Dad, I've been testing this No Fear ring for a while, and I don't feel any different," Max said with a frown. "Maybe it's defective."

"Don't put that in your report, or they won't hire you again," Mr. Russo advised his son. "They're paying you because they hope you'll say good things about the ring."

"But you always say I should be honest," Max reminded Mr. Russo.

Alex rolled her eyes. Her brother had so much left to learn. It was a good thing she was around to show him the ropes. *If* she felt like it.

"I'm not telling you to be *dishonest*," Mr. Russo said quickly. "I'm just telling you to leave out all the bad things about the ring."

Luckily Mr. Russo was saved from any further attempt to explain himself by the sound of the bell. Literally. The bell on the door chimed as Justin and Zeke walked into the restaurant. They took a seat in one of the booths lined up against the wall.

"I've got to make prom special for Juliet," Justin said as he ran his fingers nervously through his hair. "She's been to tons of them."

"Juliet's been to a lot of proms?" Zeke asked, more confused than usual.

Justin had to think fast to cover up his slip—and conceal Juliet's vampire identity. "Yeah, because she already graduated," he replied.

"An older lady?" Zeke said, sounding impressed. "Way to go, buddy! You know what they say about older ladies?"

"What?" Justin asked.

"They like to eat dinner at four," Zeke teased Justin. "And they get amazing discounts!"

Justin, however, wasn't in the mood for jokes. He was too worried about coming up with an amazing way to impress Juliet at prom. "Maybe I'll get up onstage with the DJ and serenade Juliet in front of everyone," he suggested. "Then, when the tears are welling up in her eyes, I'll ask her to go steady."

Zeke looked alarmed. "Serenade? Danger!

Danger!" he cried. This did not sound good at all. He had to save his buddy before he made an utter fool of himself. He had a much better idea. "Here's what you do—pick her up in a horse-drawn carriage. Girls love alternate means of transportation."

Justin's face brightened. Now *that* was a great idea! At that moment, Juliet walked in. He couldn't wait to tell her!

"Juliet! I know what I'm going to do!" Justin cried. "I'm going to take you to the prom in a horse-drawn carriage!"

Juliet smiled at her boyfriend—but she didn't look very enthusiastic. "Well . . ." she began. "Every time I've gone to a prom in a horse-drawn carriage, we've had to walk home."

"Oh, because the horses run away?" Zeke asked.

Juliet raised her eyebrows. "They try," she said. Then she leaned close to Justin and whispered, "But I'm too fast for them. Then it's lights out, horses!"

Justin grinned at Juliet. There was no doubt in his mind that a vampire girlfriend was the coolest kind of girlfriend ever! Although Zeke might have gotten a little nervous if he heard she liked to take out the transportation.

"You really don't have to do anything special for prom," Juliet urged.

Justin finally gave in. "Okay, no horse-drawn carriage. But I'm definitely going to serenade you at the prom."

"Oh, no one's ever done that before!" Juliet exclaimed. "That's pretty good, Justin."

"I knew it," Justin gloated.

Zeke shook his head. "I know nothing about women," he said sadly.

"I can't wait to dig up Mom and Dad and tell them!" Juliet said. Giving Justin a quick hug, she hurried out the door, back to the Late Nite Bite to find her parents. Luckily, Zeke was too busy bemoaning his lack of lady skills to hear her comment about parents . . . and digging up. That would have been a tough one to explain.

On her way out, Juliet held the door open for Harper, who was coming to see Alex. When she saw her friend walk into the restaurant, Alex immediately dropped the tomato she was slicing and went into the dining room to hang out with Harper.

Max, who was completely bored with washing lettuce, followed his sister's lead. Clearing tables was much better than prepping veggies. And sometimes people even left tips!

Alex, however, wasn't going out there to collect tips or make small talk. She had a bigger mission. Without hesitating, she nudged Harper in Zeke's direction and gave her a meaningful look.

Harper took a deep breath. It was now or never. Bracing herself, she walked over to

Zeke. This time, she was going to ask him to zombie prom. No more stalling, no more delays, no more excuses.

"Zeke, there's only one thing that will make zombie prom fun for me," Harper said, hoping her voice didn't sound as nervous as she felt. "Would you . . . design a decorative coffin table for the snacks?"

"Snack committee? Awesome," Zeke agreed at once. "I'm on it!"

Harper tried to smile back at him, then hurried back to Alex. When she was sure Zeke wasn't looking, Harper buried her head in her hands. "I did it again, Alex. I panicked and completely bailed," Harper moaned.

"Yeah, you did," Alex said bluntly. "But I think I know how to help you with your fear."

Alex walked over to Max. "Hey, Max, nice job busing that table!" she said cheerfully as she held up her hand. "High five!"

"It feels good to be appreciated," Max remarked as he high-fived Alex back.

"Yeah, don't get used to it," Alex replied. She turned around and walked back to Harper, smiling to herself.

"Put this on," Alex said as she handed Max's ring to Harper. "I borrowed it from Max. It's a magic No Fear ring."

"A No Fear ring?" Harper said nervously. "I'm a little scared."

"Yes," Alex said patiently. "Until you put it on. Plus, it totally goes with what you're wearing!"

"It does, doesn't it?" Harper asked as she slipped on the ring. As she admired it, the ring began to glow.

"Don't show anybody," Alex warned Harper. "Max doesn't even know that I took it." She couldn't risk her little brother going all bratty on her and ratting her out to the parents. They didn't like when she did this kind of thing—at all.

Harper's eyes widened. "You'd make an amazing pickpocket," she said.

"It's not a skill I'm proud of," Alex replied, trying to look ashamed.

Suddenly, a change seemed to come over Harper. Holding her head high, she strode across the restaurant to Zeke.

"Zeke. Zombie prom. Me. You. On a date," Harper said confidently. "Let's do this thing."

"All right!" Zeke said excitedly. "And Mom said no girls would like me if I spent all my time building stuff in my room. Take that, *mi madre*!"

"My mom said the same thing to me, about boys and wearing bird-themed clothing," Harper replied casually.

"No way. I love your clothes," Zeke said.

"Walk with me. And keep telling me the things you love about me," Harper ordered.

And Zeke was happy to oblige!

Alex raised her eyebrows as she watched the

new Harper in action. It looked like the No Fear ring worked, after all.

Suddenly, a small pit of fear took root in Alex's stomach. Had it worked a little *too* well?

Chapter Four

Soon, the big night had arrived: it was time for the Tribeca Prep prom at last! And for Alex, Harper, and Zeke, that meant that it was time for the zombie prom. Justin and Alex rushed through their shifts at the Waverly Sub Station so that they would have enough time to get ready.

Alex usually didn't need to spend much time on her hair and makeup; messing with a bunch of cosmetics and styling products wasn't really her style. But she usually didn't have to get all dressed up as a zombie, either. For zombie prom, Alex wanted to make sure that her zombie look was as realistic as possible.

Justin decided that he would need to multitask in order to get everything done in time. As he set some tables, Justin warmed up his vocal cords so that he wouldn't hit any wrong notes during his serenade for Juliet that night.

"Me, me, me, me, me, me, me, me," Justin sang. "I, I, I, I, I, I, I, I."

"You are *so* self-centered," Alex laughed as she refilled the ketchup bottles.

"I'm doing vocal exercises so I can serenade Juliet tonight," Justin explained.

"Singing? In front of all those people?" Alex asked. "Who do you think you are, Li'l Galileo?"

"Hey, I can sing!" Justin said defensively.

"Oh, I know you can sing," replied Alex.

"I'm just saying, do you really want to do it in front of *all* those people, looking right up at you? Waving their cell phone cameras. Taking your picture. Putting it on the Internet so that people can watch it for years and years and years."

Justin tried to act cool, but in truth, Alex was starting to scare him. He hadn't really thought through the consequences of his serenade. The Internet could really damage a reputation. Then he shook his head to clear the negative thoughts. "No, it's going to be great, because I'm also going to ask her to go steady with me," he said, sounding more confident than he felt.

"Go steady?" Alex cracked up. "Whose prom are you going to? Grandpa's?"

"Going steady is romantic," Justin insisted.

Alex nodded. "If you find hysterical laughter romantic, you're good," she replied.

"I'm not nervous, Alex," Justin said

stubbornly. He figured that as long as she couldn't see his shaky hands, she might believe him.

"I didn't ask, but thanks," Alex replied, still giggling.

As soon as Alex had turned away, Justin ran into the kitchen, where he found Max grating some cheese.

"Max, listen, I need to borrow your No Fear ring tonight," Justin said urgently.

"Fine, but this thing doesn't work," Max said. "I don't feel the least bit different." He raised his hand to take off the ring—and finally noticed that it was gone. "Oh. Maybe that's why I don't feel different."

"Max, where's the ring?" Justin said.

"I don't know," Max said, shrugging. "I must have lost it. Check my ear. I have my finger in there a lot."

But Justin was too upset to even consider digging around in Max's ear for the No Fear ring. "I won't have the nerve to serenade Juliet without that ring!" he said as panic crept into his voice. "And how in the world am I going to ask her to go steady?"

"'Go steady?'" Max repeated, laughing. "Who are you, Grandpa?"

"Oh, man!" Justin moaned. "I promised her I'd sing to her, but without that ring I'm scared to death!"

"You know what you can do instead?" Max said, trying to be helpful.

Justin turned to Max, hoping with his whole heart that for once, Max would have a plan that made sense—instead of the usual wacky, insane plots he hatched.

"Bring in one of those aboveground pools, fill it with fruit punch, give everybody scuba gear, and the bubbles from the scuba tanks turn that thing into a huge cherry soda," Max suggested cheerfully. "Now, *that's* a great prom!"

Justin closed his eyes and tried to stay calm. His hopes had clearly been in vain. Opening his eyes, he looked straight at Max. "We're done talking."

Now Justin just had to come up with a whole new brilliant plan. In no time. With no magic.

He sighed. Why was life so difficult?

Chapter Five

Just a few hours later, Juliet, Harper, and Zeke came over to the Russos' loft to take pictures before the two proms. Justin couldn't believe how gorgeous Juliet looked in her elegant formal gown. He only hoped that he looked half as handsome in the fancy tuxedo he had rented!

The rest of the group didn't look quite so beautiful—but they were certainly terrifying!

Alex, Harper, and Zeke were wearing ghoulish makeup so that their skin looked pasty and white, with dark circles under their eyes. Alex's and Harper's dresses were shredded and tattered. And Zeke's tux looked like something he had borrowed from a dead guy.

"All right, you all look so great!" Mr. Russo exclaimed as he walked into the room with a camera. "I want to take a picture. Let's line up from deadest to least dead."

"I'm dead inside," Alex announced. "So I'll be on this end."

"Zeke, put your arm around my shoulder," Harper ordered him. "I won't bite."

Zeke immediately did what Harper said. "I don't want to come on too strong," he explained apologetically.

"A piece of advice if you're going to be my prom date: man up," Harper replied. The ring was apparently still in full force.

Zeke looked at her with admiration as he

leaned over to Justin and whispered, "Feisty. Me likey!"

But Harper was shocked at her own behavior. She turned to Alex, a worried look on her face. "Is there a way to dial this ring down a little?" she asked softly.

"Yeah, take it off," Alex said. "You're only supposed to wear it when you need it."

Harper's eyes flashed. That was not the answer she wanted. "Just try to get it off!" she hissed. "I'll take you down!"

Alex stepped back. Normally, she could handle Harper with no trouble at all. But the No Fear ring had changed that!

Oblivious, Mr. Russo held the camera up to his face. He counted down, "And three, two, one!"

Flash!

A bright light from the camera's flash filled the room.

Juliet felt a searing pain in her eyes from the

brightness of the flash—like any light-sensitive vampire would. She covered her eyes with her hands and hissed, revealing her sharp fangs. "Ugh! That flash blinded me!" she complained.

"My eyes were closed. Take another one," Harper called out.

Flash!

This time, Juliet used her extreme vampire speed to zoom over to Mr. Russo and grab the camera away from him. "No more pictures," she said firmly.

"Wait," Zeke said. He looked confused. "She was just over there."

Justin tried to cover up Juliet's superspeed. "No, man. You fell asleep," he replied.

"Aw, I hate it when that happens!" Zeke complained. "What year is it?"

Juliet crossed the room and stood next to Justin again. "Look, I already have a picture of me in this prom dress," she said quietly.

"Painted by da Vinci when I went to prom with him."

"*Leonardo* da Vinci?" Justin asked. "Can we get through this without bringing up *all* of your old boyfriends?"

"All right, guys!" Mr. Russo announced, clapping his hands. "Go out and have your best night ever!"

"We will!" Juliet said, grinning. "Justin's going to serenade me!"

Justin stifled a groan. "Right. You remembered," he said. He'd been hoping she hadn't.

Noticing her brother's expression, Alex smiled evilly. "Oh, she almost forgot—but I've been reminding her a lot!" she teased Justin. That was what younger sisters were for, right?

The pictures taken and the good-byes said, the group left the loft. The friends walked to Tribeca Prep together, and when they reached the school, they split into two groups. Justin and Juliet headed off to the cafeteria, where the regular prom was being held. Alex, Harper, and Zeke went to the gym for the zombie prom.

Alex had helped plan the zombie prom, so she knew exactly what to expect when she walked into the gym. Even so, she was really impressed with the transformation from gym to spooky cemetery, complete with misty clouds of dry ice. Ghoulish black streamers hung from the walls. A banner above the door read WORST NIGHT EVER. At the far end of the gym, a long table was piled high with scary-looking snacks. It even had a punch bowl in the shape of a skull, with bloodred punch sloshing around inside it!

And the turnout was great! Alex wasn't surprised, though. She knew people would rather go to a zombie prom than some awful, boring, normal prom. What she hadn't expected was everybody's dedication to creating authentic-looking costumes for zombie prom.

The other kids had truly outdone themselves!

Alex turned to Harper. "How great is this!" she exclaimed proudly. "We all look gross, no one's smiling, and we get to drink brains!"

As the three friends walked over to the punch bowl, Zeke tapped Harper's shoulder. "You look beautiful tonight," he said shyly.

"I look beautiful?" Harper asked. "How do you think that's supposed to make me feel? I'm *trying* to look like a zombie."

Zeke shook his head. "You look gross," he corrected.

"Too little, too late," Harper snapped.

Alex rolled her eyes as she got in line for a glass of punch. The No Fear ring seemed to be growing more powerful the longer Harper wore it! This could be a problem. She'd have to deal with it—after the prom, of course.

Just then, a couple slowly lumbered up to the refreshment table. Alex didn't recognize either of them as students at Tribeca Prep. And there was something about them that wasn't quite right.

"Do I have any brains in my teeth?" the guy asked.

"Yes," replied the girl.

"Cool," said the guy.

Another strange kid came up to the table then and slowly tried to cut in front of Harper in line.

"Hey, no cutsies," Harper barked. She turned to Zeke and said, "His costume is weak, but the smell is right on."

The kid turned around and stared at Harper. His eyes were rolled all the way back in his head, revealing only the white parts.

"Wow—great white contact lenses, man," Alex said approvingly. "Way to commit."

"Why don't you shuffle yourself to the back of the line, buddy?" Harper suggested.

"Uh, Harper, maybe we should let him cut in front of us," Zeke suggested nervously as the guy began to growl. "He seems a little dehydrated . . . and not in the mood to talk."

"Zeke, how can you be so cute and so spineless at the same time?" Harper demanded. "I'm going to stand up to this punk!"

Suddenly, the kid's arm fell off! He slowly reached down to pick it up.

"This isn't brain punch," complained another strange boy. "There's nothing chewy in it."

"*They* look chewy," his date said, staring right at Alex, Harper, and Zeke with lifeless eyes.

"Real zombies," Alex whispered. Suddenly, everything made sense—all the strange kids she didn't recognize, their weird smells, their incredibly authentic zombie costumes.

And the guy whose arm had fallen off—that made sense, too, now that she realized he was a zombie! This was not good. Not good at all.

"Uh, Harper, Zeke, I think we should get

out of here," Alex said urgently.

"You, too?" Harper said loudly. "Doesn't anyone have any guts around here?"

Alex did *not* have time to deal with No Fear Harper right now. She turned to Zeke. "Zeke, I'll be right back," she said. "Stay with Harper. You're her date."

"I'm starting to question that decision," Zeke replied, as he watched Alex dash out the door.

Chapter Six

Alex ran through the halls of Tribeca Prep as fast as she could until she reached the cafeteria, where the regular prom was being held. The prom committee had transformed the cafeteria into a beautiful room filled with flowers, balloons, streamers, and a huge banner that declared BEST NIGHT EVER! in giant letters. They'd even managed to somehow get rid of the cafeteria smell.

As Alex burst into the cafeteria, Justin was nervously walking up the steps to the stage. The room was quiet as he picked up the microphone. "Let's hear it for the best night ever!" Justin yelled into the mic, trying to pump up the crowd.

But everyone just stared at him in silence.

"Anyway, I guess I'd like to invite Juliet Van Heusen up onstage," Justin continued.

Juliet smiled shyly as she gracefully climbed the stairs to stand next to Justin. The room erupted in whistles and catcalls from the guys.

"Hey, come on, guys, she's my date!" Justin protested. "Before I announce the winner of the table centerpiece raffle, I would like to sing to her."

A girl in the audience grabbed her date's arm. "Oh, my gosh, he's going to sing to her!" she squealed. Then her face grew stern. "Don't you *ever* do that to me."

Justin pressed a couple buttons on his

cell phone, then held it up to the mic. A cheesy electronic drum loop played over the speakers.

Alex couldn't wipe the huge grin off her face. Zombie crisis aside, Alex couldn't believe her luck: the chance to see Justin make a major fool of himself at prom was priceless—and worth leaving the zombies alone for a few more minutes. "How's that for perfect timing?" she asked herself.

Justin cleared his throat and began to sing—not just any song, but one that he'd composed and written himself!

I'm too nervous to be clever
But I'd do anything for you—whatever,
To be without you, I'd say, "Never!"
It's because you and I are together
That makes this the best night ever.

As Justin finished singing, there was silence in the cafeteria. Juliet tried to smile supportively at him—and not cringe from the complete and total awkwardness—but it wasn't easy.

One of the guys in the audience turned to his date and asked, "Could this get any worse?"

As much as Alex would have enjoyed reveling in Justin's humiliation for a little while longer, she knew that she had to deal with the zombie situation. Hopefully, the zombies hadn't attacked her friends yet. Maybe it was a good thing that zombies were so slow. And if only Zeke could get No Fear Harper to stop being so fearless . . .

Alex shook her head and focused. She needed help to beat the zombies. And that help would have to come from her incredibly dorky older brother, whether he wanted to give it or not.

Then again, she figured, Justin was probably looking for an excuse to escape from the scene of his embarrassment. At least, she hoped he was!

As Alex pushed through the crowd to reach the stage, she realized that Justin wasn't quite done humiliating himself yet. He reached for Juliet's hand as he said into the microphone, "I'd like to say one more thing. Juliet, would you go steady with me?"

Even Alex cringed. Some of the kids at the prom started to laugh, while others just looked confused.

"'Go steady?'" a guy asked his date. "What does that even mean?"

"I don't know," she replied. "I'm going to call my grandpa and ask."

Alex raced up the stairs to the stage, where Justin was blushing and looking miserable. She leaned close to her brother and whispered, "Justin, real zombies have crashed zombie prom."

But Justin shook his head. "I can't hear you," he replied.

Alex leaned in closer—not noticing the microphone, which was still on. "Real zombies have crashed zombie prom," she said.

Her voice boomed through the cafeteria, blaring through every speaker! The audience gasped.

A look of horror crossed Alex's face. "Oh, my gosh!" she said. "Uh, a lot of you might think you heard me say 'real zombies,'" she said, trying to cover up her goof. "But it's a zombie prom, so I say 'zombies' a lot. Like I just said it a bunch of times right there. That is all."

Alex thrust the mic at Justin. "Help!" she pleaded.

Justin took the microphone and said calmly, "What she meant to say is the band Real Zombies is playing at the zombie prom."

There was a murmur of excitement and then the crowd began leaving in waves. They were heading to the zombie prom!

Alex stared at Justin. Had a zombie already

gotten his brain? That was the only excuse she could think of that would explain how dumb that announcement had been. They wanted to keep people *away* from the zombies—not open up an all-you-can-eat brain buffet!

"Cool!" Juliet said, as unaware as the rest of the student population just how uncool it really was. "I want to go get a T-shirt."

"No!" Alex cried. "They're *real* zombies, slowly creeping in on Harper and Zeke!"

"Too bad," Justin said sadly. "I really liked that guy."

"Juliet, you're a vampire," Alex said urgently. "You could bite the zombies." It seemed like a very practical solution.

But Juliet shook her head. "Sure, if you want stronger, faster zombies," she replied.

"Probably not the way to go," Justin said.

Alex sighed as she grabbed Justin and Juilet's hands and pulled them down the steps. There was not a moment to lose!

Chapter Seven

Back at the zombie prom, Harper was in trouble. Big trouble. Although she didn't quite realize it yet.

The crowd of zombies had increased dramatically—but No Fear Harper still thought she could take them on. While she picked a fight with one zombie, another slowly approached her from the side. Harper spun around to confront him.

"What are you looking at?" she demanded.

"I want to have you for dinner," the zombie muttered.

"I have a date, jerk," Harper shot back.

But where *was* her date? Harper scanned the gym. "Zeke?" she called.

Zeke poked his head out from beneath the DJ's table. "Under here!" he whispered.

Harper got up in the zombie's face. "Now you've made my date uncomfortable!" she yelled. "And you're going to apologize, or else you're going to meet the king and queen of this prom!"

Harper shook her right fist in the zombie's face. "That was the king." she said. Then she held up her left fist. "And that was the queen!"

Just then, Alex, Justin, and Juliet burst into the room. Justin took one look at the crowd of zombies surrounding Harper and yelled, "Where's Zeke?"

Alex and Juliet searched the room, but they didn't see him.

Justin knew there was one way to find his buddy. He called out in a strange, alien-sounding language.

Once again, Zeke poked his head out from under the DJ's table. He responded to Justin in the same weird alien-talk. Then he switched to English. "Justin, you are a sight for sore eyes!" Zeke exclaimed. "Harper's standing up to those creeps. She's fearless!"

"Got any room under there?" Justin asked urgently as he lifted the tablecloth. Then he noticed the dirty look Juliet was giving him. "Um, for Juliet, I mean."

"I'm good," Juliet replied.

As if things couldn't get more out of control, at that moment Max burst into the room. He slammed the doors shut behind him.

"Max, save yourself!" Justin called. "This place is infested with zombies."

"I know," replied Max. "I got an RSVP from some zombies."

"So *that's* where the fliers went," Alex said. She was going to get Max for this. Big-time.

"Yeah!" Max continued. "Zombies are coming. But don't worry, I already locked the doors. Nobody can get in, and we can't get out!"

Justin and Alex exchanged a glance. Max clearly didn't get it that the zombies were *already* inside. But maybe it was better that he didn't understand the grave danger they were facing.

"Did you at least find the No Fear ring?" Justin asked his little brother. "I could really use it right now."

"Harper has it," Alex spoke up. "That's why she's standing up to the zombies."

"Harper has my ring?" Max asked, perking up. "I'm going in! Make sure to warn me if the zombies show up. Oh, right, the doors are locked. I'm sure we're fine!"

Max walked over to Harper, passing by the

crowd of zombies that were still slowly trying to surround her.

"I've always wondered—how does anyone get caught by zombies?" Juliet asked.

"It's usually if they're running and they trip over a rock," Justin answered. "Or their car won't start."

"Excuse me. Pardon me. Coming through," Max said politely as he passed by the zombies. At last he reached Harper. "Harper, you've got to give me my ring back. See, I'm a product tester and I need to file a report on it in order to get paid."

Harper shooed Max away. "Not now," she replied. Then she turned to the zombies. "You can't scare me!"

Alex groaned. This was like something out of a horrible comedy of errors.

And then it got worse.

Across the room, a strange look crossed Juliet's face. Justin looked closely at her. "Why are your fangs out?" he asked.

"I thought I saw blood on that zombie," she replied, licking her lips. "Hold me back! I'm about to go into a blood frenzy!"

"It's old, dead zombie blood," Justin tried to reason with her. "That can't taste good."

"You're right," Juliet said as she took a deep breath. "Thanks for talking me down."

"You guys!" Alex yelled. "We've got to help Harper!"

She dragged Zeke out from under the DJ table. Together with Justin and Juliet, they charged into the crowd of zombies to save Harper . . . and Max, maybe.

"Harper, we're taking you out of here," Alex said firmly as she grabbed her friend's arm.

Harper just shook Alex off. "I'm not afraid of these losers!" she shouted.

The zombies started to close in around Alex, Harper, Zeke, Justin, Juliet, and Max.

Alex wished she could get the No Fear ring away from Harper—because she felt like she was about to panic!

Zeke frowned as he got a closer look at the zombies. "If I didn't know better, I'd say these zombie promgoers are real zombies," he said.

"They're, uh, from another school's drama department," Alex said as she tried to cover up the truth about the zombies. "They have an unbelievable costume designer who also teaches chorus."

Zeke nodded. That made sense. "They must be here to dance-battle us!" he said.

One of the zombie boys stopped. "Dance battle?" he asked. "We do love to dance."

"It's on!" Zeke announced.

A zombie girl sighed. "One music video and we're expected to have dance battles everywhere," she complained.

But the rest of the zombies were ready to

show off their best dance moves. They slowly moved into a triangle formation across from the kids. Justin ran across the gym to the DJ table and put on a CD. Then he joined the nonzombie dance team. The two groups faced off, ready to dance.

They started with a one-on-one dance battle. First Alex danced against a zombie. She was soon followed by Justin, Juliet, Harper, Zeke, and Max, all of them dancing as best they could. And even though some of them—like Justin—weren't very good dancers, they were worlds better than the zombies, who moved so slowly they couldn't keep up with the beat. And the zombies' arms and legs kept falling off, which made it even harder for them to feel the rhythm.

After the individual dance battles, the teams assembled for a final group performance. As the tempo of the music picked up, the kids danced faster and faster. The zombies just couldn't keep up. They collapsed in a pile of bodies, arms, and legs!

"We won!" cheered the kids, jumping up and down and clapping.

The zombies knew that they had been beaten. They groaned as they tried to attach their fallen arms and legs. Then they slowly dragged themselves off toward the doors to go back home to the cemetery.

"Just once I'd like to win one of these," grumbled a zombie boy.

"That's right, keep walking, zombies!" Max hollered after them. "What kind of zombies can't even do the zombie dance?"

"Shhh!" Alex hissed at her little brother. "Max, they're zombies. They could come back and eat your brain."

But that didn't seem to bother Max one bit. "Good luck trying to eat *these* brains, zombies!" he yelled as he tapped his head. "My dad says I have a thick skull!"

Justin turned to Alex, nodding toward their little brother. "He doesn't have the ring on, but he's still not afraid of anything," he said.

"Maybe there's something wrong with the ring," Alex replied. "But when Harper wore it, she had no fear."

"Oh, my gosh!" Justin exclaimed as he realized what was going on. "It doesn't work on Max, because Max already has no fear!"

"Everybody has fear," Alex argued. She and Justin looked at Max.

"Hey, who wants to dare me to cannonball into that punchbowl?" Max shouted. "Ah, you don't have to dare me. I dare myself!"

"Okay," Alex said, admitting that Justin was right. "He has no fear."

As Max climbed onto the refreshment table, Harper ran over to Alex. She gestured at the huge crowd of regular promgoers who had crashed the zombie prom. "Alex, looks like anti-prom was more popular than real prom," Harper said.

"Wait," Alex said, holding up her hand. "That means that next year, more people will want to go to anti-prom."

"So then we'll go to real prom," Harper replied.

Alex nodded. "We're always one step ahead of them!" she said.

Zeke walked up to the girls, carrying a zombie foot. "Anyone in here lose a foot?" he asked. "This thing is unbelievably real. That chorus teacher is talented!"

Alex just shook her head. Then she walked over to the refreshment table so she could grab a glass of punch before Max went swimming in it.

Chapter Eight

Late that night, after the zombie prom had ended, the gym was almost empty. Nearly all the promgoers had gone home. The zombies were back in the cemetery. Only Juliet was left, sitting alone, waiting for Justin. At last, he rushed in carrying a CD.

"Where have you been?" Juliet asked.

"I had to run home and grab this," Justin said breathlessly. "It's our song." He popped the CD into the player. A beautiful slow-tempo melody filled the room.

With a smile, Justin held out his hand to Juliet. The two began to slow-dance in the empty gym.

"You really know how to dance," Justin complimented Juliet. "How many zombie proms have you been to?"

Juliet looked up at Justin and stared into his brown eyes. "Yes," she replied.

"Yes?" he asked, sounding confused. That didn't really answer his question. . . .

"Yes, I will go steady with you," Juliet continued.

"You will!" exclaimed Justin. "That's great, because people sort of indicated it was lame—but I don't care what they think, because I'm nuts about you and all I want to do is make you happy."

With a smile, Justin leaned in to kiss Juliet. And he wasn't even wearing the No Fear ring.

"*This* is the best night ever," Juliet said with a sigh as she rested her head on Justin's shoulder.

Splash!

Suddenly, Justin and Juliet were drenched by a wave of red fruit punch!

"Nailed it!" Max yelled as he came up for air from the perfect dive into the punch bowl.

But for once in his life, Justin wasn't mad at Max for performing yet another one of his crazy stunts. Nothing could upset him now, with Juliet by his side, smiling up at him in that special way that made Justin feel like the coolest, smartest, most amazing guy in the world. He gave Juliet another kiss. And without needing her to say it, Justin could tell that out of all the proms Juliet had ever been to, this one was her favorite—despite the awkward serenade, the public request to go steady, the zombie attack, and even the fruit-punch tidal wave.

And that was all Justin had wanted!

Something magical is on the way!
Look for the next book in Disney's
Wizards of Waverly Place series.

Oh, Brother!

Adapted by Sarah Nathan

Based on the series created by Todd J. Greenwald

Based on the episode, "Justin's Little Sister," Written by Eve Weston

Alex Russo sat in Mr. Laritate's social studies class, talking to her best friend, Harper Evans. She kept her eye on the door, waiting for their teacher to walk in. Just as the bell rang, he entered the classroom. He was dressed in his usual suit, but instead of a regular necktie he was wearing a bolo tie, a traditional cowboy neckpiece. "All right, my little history wranglers, enough ruckus!" Mr. Laritate bellowed.

"Let's start off Thursday's class as we always do." He paused and waited for his usual punch line. "With an oral pop quiz!"

All the students groaned. Alex turned to Harper, who was sitting behind her. "Oh, my gosh," she said sarcastically. "It's the Thursday pop quiz we have *every* Thursday. I'm totally caught off guard." She rolled her eyes at her friend.

Mr. Laritate scanned the classroom for his first victim. "In no particular order," he said, "Wendy Bott, you're up! The French and Indian War was fought by three groups of people. Name two of them."

Wendy stood up and fidgeted nervously. "Um . . . the French was one for sure," she stuttered. "And the other one . . . I'm just going to guess, Indians?"

Mr. Laritate grinned. "Excellent!" he exclaimed as he rang the large cowbell sitting on his desk. He called on the next student.

"Nellie Rodriguez, you're up. The War of eighteen twelve started in what year?"

"Oh, my gosh," Nellie said nervously. "I studied for this one." She quickly looked down at her hand where she had written the answer. "Uh . . . eighteen twelve?"

Once again, Mr. Laritate rang his bell. "Another winner!" Suddenly, he zoned in on Alex. "Alex Russo," he said. "The Monroe Doctrine. What is it? When was it passed? And please give a two-minute argument defending it."

Alex couldn't believe it. Everyone else had gotten such easy questions! This was totally unfair.

"Hold on," she said as she stood up. "The other two questions had the answers *in* them. My question's supposed to be: the Monroe Doctrine—whose doctrine is it? I'd say 'Monroe' and you'd say, "Yipee-dilly-willy way-to-go-little-filly.'"

"Oh, Alex," groaned Mr. Laritate, shaking his head disapprovingly. "You are *definitely* not your brother Justin."

"No, I'm not," Alex agreed. "I'm cuter and more fun to talk to. And I don't have dental floss on a key chain."

Mr. Laritate grinned and reached for something in his pocket. "Yeah, well, I do!" he exclaimed, pulling out a key chain that had dental floss hanging from it. "Justin made it for me." Mr. Laritate let out a sigh. "Ah, Justin. Those were the days."

As Alex sat down, she turned back to Harper. "Can you believe this?" she asked. "He's comparing me to Justin!"

"I know. It is so hard to live up to Justin," Harper said sympathetically. Then she got a dreamy look on her face as she thought about him. "He's smart and handsome, and he has the *healthiest* gums. I mean—"

Alex held up her hand. "Okay, I get it! He

flosses. Let's make him president!" She turned back around in her seat and slumped down in her chair. This was going to be a long social studies class!

In the kitchen of the Waverly Sub Station, the restaurant that the Russo family owned and ran, Mrs. Russo put on her apron. She was getting ready to prepare some sandwiches just as Alex and Justin walked in.

"How was school today?" she asked. She looked at Alex and then over at Justin. "Wait, let me guess. Who got in trouble?" she commented, looking directly at her daughter once again. She knew full well that Alex had a tendency to always get into some sort of trouble.

Justin smirked as Alex reached over to open the freezer door. The door actually opened into the Wizard's Lair, the room where Mr. Russo gave Alex and her brothers wizard lessons every Tuesday and Thursday after school. Each of the Russo children had magic powers and they were all wizards-in-training. Their dad had given up his wizard powers, when he married their mom, a nonwizard. Now he gave lessons to his kids so that they would be prepared for the family wizard competition when they turned eighteen. Only one of the Russo kids would win and remain a wizard, so the stakes were seriously high.

Alex sighed and turned back to her mom. "Well, I got a hard quiz question because of Justin," she complained, "got in trouble because of Justin, and got recruited by the math team because of Justin." She turned and headed into the lair. Life would be a whole lot easier without Justin around, Alex thought woefully.

Mrs. Russo raised her eyebrows at Justin, who was looking smug. "What are you smiling about?" she asked.

"I have had a much more productive day than I realized," he gloated.